Carnival of the Undead

My Life Among the Undead:

Book 4

Camara M. Bragdon

My Life Among the Undead

book series

Friend of the Undead

Yard Sale of the Undead

Secrets of the Undead

DEDICATION

This book is dedicated to my parents, Randy and Judy Bragdon. Thanks for always being there for me.

CONTENTS

Chapter One:
I Get My Own Personal Stalker

I had no idea how long the guy had been staring at me.

Allow me to set the scene for you. I'm an assistant librarian at the Zephyr Public Library. One of my many duties is shelving books, which is what I was doing on the third floor in the fiction section when I saw him. I was down on one knee putting away a few novels on the bottom shelf when I got a feeling I was being watched. I looked up to see him staring intently at me.

He was a short, balding man. I pegged him to be in his mid-forties, but since Zephyr is a city full of myth and magic, it was hard to tell his exact age. Many people can live for centuries without looking old at all. Take my boyfriend, for example. If you didn't know him, you would think he was in his mid-twenties when, in fact, he is really sixty-five. But don't tell him I said that.

Plus, I'm really crappy at telling people's ages.

The weirdo wore a red and white trucker's cap and a black trench coat. I hoped to God he wasn't planning on flashing me. Yes, that's exactly what I needed to brighten my day.

As nonchalantly as I could manage, I grabbed the metal cart loaded with books waiting to be reshelved and pushed it to the next section of fiction in the next room. A few moments later, the same guy was staring at me again from the next aisle over. That's a little odd, I thought, Maybehe's just following the same pattern as me. I remembered seeing him at the library a few days earlier, but he wasn't acting like this before.

I decided to play it safe and moved to the other side of the room where I began shelving furiously in the biographies section. Glancing over my shoulder, I noticed the stranger pawing through the books. If he didn't keep staring at me, you would think he was just browsing. My subconscious thought produced a tidal wave of red flags. The cart had only six books left on it. If I just acted casual, I could double my shelving record in no time. I turned on my heel and quickly gathered up the rest of the books from the cart.

Everywhere I went, the man was right in my line of vision. I could almost hear my heart pounding against my rib cage. Uncle Creepy was constantly looking at me. Don't freak out, I told myself. Maybe, he's just looking at the books in the same area where you happen to be. My suspicions were confirmed when he dropped onto one knee at the exact time I did. I shoved the book in place. At this moment, I could care less if some patron couldn't find that particular book on great places to go manticore hunting. My main priority was getting away from this freak!

I grabbed the cart and practically sprinted towards the elevator. Glancing over my shoulder, I saw him walking a few paces behind me. Like a scene from a bad horror movie, the elevator came after the hundredth time pushing of the down button. The doors had barely opened when the cart and I dove inside. I frantically searched for the "Door Close" button. Why don't they use bright colors and a name like "Close the Door on Creeps" button?

The guy attempted to board the elevator with me, but there was no way in Hell I was going to let that happen. My only weapon was the cart, and I positioned it in front of me. If he was trying to intimidate me, he was doing a pretty good job. He never saw the cart ram into his legs as he grabbed one of the handles. A sharp cry of pain exploded from his lips as he crumpled to the floor in agony.

I pulled the cart back into the safety of the elevator. Once the door closed, I leaned against the wall and placed my hand over my chest. I had heard stories about people stalking librarians in the stacks, but I never thought it would ever happen to me. Never say never, I guess. My heart rate returned to normal by the time I had arrived in the back office.

"Shelly, what happened to you?" my werewolf supervisor, Raquel Lupus, asked as she looked up from her mounting pile of paperwork. In her human form, she is a beautiful woman with olive skin and long, silky black hair which was pulled back in a French braid behind her tufted, pointed ears.

"I just had a terrifying experience up in the stacks!" I then proceeded to tell her what had transpired in the last fifteen minutes. "I probably should've just left the books on the cart, but I wasn't sure if he was actually following me or not. He was short, balding—I think—I couldn't really tell because he was wearing a red trucker cap. And no, I don't know if he was drunk or not," I said, answering her unspoken question. "I tried not to get too close to him."

To answer your question, yes, I did read her mind. Every human, like me, receives a superpower when they leave their reality and come into Zephyr. My power of telepathy is limited, allowing me to be read-only the minds of the undead, and werewolves fall into that category. It's the magical gift I acquired when I first arrived in this strange, strange world a few years back.

"Well," Raquel said, "I'm going to call Tito up here!" She picked up the phone and dialed the custodians' extension. I walked over to stare at the work schedule on the bulletin board as she spoke to a member of our janitor/security team. I felt a little bit relieved that Tito Enano was on duty today. Looks can be deceiving, especially here in Zephyr. Tito Enano is tall for a dwarf, averaging a good three-and-half-feet tall, but don't let that fool you. The ex-Special Ops officer can kick your butt any day of the week with his solid body.

Tito was standing in the office with his beefy arms crossed listening intently as I told him what had happened. "I'll go take a quick search of the building," he said in an accent similar to that of a Cuban-American. With a nod of approval, he went on his mission. Raquel had me stuff envelopes with overdue notices while the dwarf looked for my stalker. Tito came back perp-less. Apparently, the man had disappeared from the library.

I was shaking from the whole ordeal, and certainly didn't want to shelve up on the third floor stacks any time soon. I asked Raquel if there was any shelving to be done on the second floor.

She shook her head. "You can do mail." Doing mail has nothing to do with sending professional letters to our patrons. In fact, it consists of pulling books off the shelves and sending them to various libraries who have sent book requests to us.

"Sure, I can handle that," I replied as I gathered up the stack of papers on a purple tray. I quickly sorted mail numerically and then went to gather the books. I liked being alone because it gave me the chance to sort out what had just happened. The papers were shaking violently in my hands as I told myself to calm down. It could have been worse. The guy could have attacked me! And if he had tried, he wouldn't have made it out in one piece.

I found myself glancing around to make sure Uncle Creepy wasn't peeking at me behind one of the bookcases. As my thoughts returned to my job, I immediately noticed five pieces of pale blue paper scattered across the floor of the very last aisle. I squatted down and scooped them up as a frown spread across my face. Whoever had taken these books didn't do a great job tearing along the edge of the book pockets. Why do people have this urge to steal library books? If you have a library card they're free to use, for Pete's sake!

I secretly hoped the cops would catch the thieves and lynch them from the highest tree. I glanced at the different titles as I walked back to the front desk so I could mark them as stolen on the library's computer system.

The first book was called The Complete Idiot's Guide to Dragon Keeping. My brother got his copy of this book when he bought his green and black dragon. The second book, Wild and Wacky Weather, made me shudder as I thought about the problems that book had given me almost six months ago. The next two were murder mysteries written by a famous elf living right in Zephyr. The very last book was called On Necromancy written by someone named Archibald Hawthorne. Sitting at the office computers, I scanned the barcode on each pocket and labeled them as lost. I was secretly ticked off at the thief who just caused the library to lose about fifty druci (the equivalent of an American dollar.)

Chapter Two:
Even Vampires Deal with Stress at Work

Around seven o'clock that evening, I headed over to the diner that my dad owns on Friendship Street. The street is really the best place for a family restaurant like Anderson's Place. The diner's motto is "a place to enjoy great food and great friendship." Heck, I probably wouldn't even be dating my boyfriend if Dad had never hired him to run the ice cream bar that's located in the back of the diner.

Dad had renovated the diner to make it look like the inside of a log cabin. I walked through the front glass doors and immediately inhaled the scent of Dad's famous sour cream apple pie. It was actually my mom's recipe, but Dad had improved it with a cup of pureed apporange, a special kind of fruit that tastes like an apple and an orange.

Fortunately, it was a slow night, and I was happy to see my brother, Robin, and two of his friends playing pool at the billiards table which had been donated by the generous vampire, Count Konrad Von Stoker.

"Yo, Shelly!" twenty-seven-year-old Robin Anderson called out to me just as he sank a ball into a side pocket. He was off work in what he calls his 'civvies,' an untucked t-shirt and a pair of worn jeans, or "It's your turn, Strider," my brother told the satyr who was drinking a cola.

The young satyr spun his cue stick around right after he adjusted the blue and gray Rasta cap that covered his two curved horns. Strider Hornsby sent the white ball into the cluster of colored balls, sending three of them into two of the pockets. He wiped his hands on the sides of his jeans, a strange ritual he always does whenever he makes a winning shot playing pool.

"One more shot like that, Strider, and you win again for the seventh time in a row!" said the vampire, Dirk Van Helsing. He took his time debating on whether or not to use his levitation spell to make the balls go into the pockets if he didn't make the shot.

Apparently, he intended to throw his moral compass right out the window in a game with a stated no-magic rule. The no magic rule was established after I had read Dirk and my boyfriend's minds and attempted to screw up their game.

"Dirk's cheating!" I announced just to annoy my boyfriend's brother, "He's going to use a levitation spell to force the balls into the pockets because he can't make this impossible shot."

Dirk shot a dirty look at me with his green eyes. "You're so dead." The tone in his voice was somewhat playful, not sincere. Even though he is a vampire, Dirk abhors violence. I believe that's one of the reasons he is a vegan.

"Please, you couldn't even hurt a fly, Dirk," I heard my boyfriend say. I turned around to see the curly, black-haired vampire carrying one end of a brightly colored jukebox. He winked one of his gorgeous green eyes at me and nearly dropped the awkward object. "Besides, Shelly can kick your skinny butt any day."

"Eddie, pay attention!" growled Bruce Miller as he got a better grip on the bottom of the jukebox. "Timothy paid the Count a lot of money for this. I should've had your brother help me instead."

"Sorry, Mr. Miller," Eddie apologized with just a hint of insincerity. He had promised me to try to get along with my dad's old friend, but so far there had been little success. They set the music machine down only a few feet away from the end of the ice cream counter.

I took a quick look at the jukebox. "Wow, it's going to be really bright when you plug it in! You'll probably have to wear shades when you're at work, Eddie."

Eddie shot me a fanged grin. He squatted down beside the forty-five-year-old cook. "Anything I can help with?" he asked. The last thing he wanted was my father to fire him because he disrespected one of my father's closest friends.

"No!" Bruce growled. Then he said in a much kinder tone, "Dirk, you think you can help me figure out all these wires? I don't want to short circuit any of the computer's wires."

"Sure," Dirk replied, "Strider's going to win anyway." He set his cue stick back on the rack Dad had installed on the wall. He brushed back a lock of his long, straight black hair and knelt down beside Bruce. They began yammering away about wires and computer jargon.

Straightening himself up, Eddie jammed his hands into the pockets of the black jeans that accentuated his cute butt. My boyfriend backed away from the two men and walked towards me. He gave me a kiss on the lips. "So, how was your day at work, babe?" he asked, not really wanting to talk about the anger he was feeling at the moment.

"Good," I replied, returning the kiss. "I found some stolen books, and someone was following me!" I said nonchalantly as I boosted myself onto one of the red leather bar stools.

Robin and Strider both looked up from their game. "Someone actually stole a library book?" my brother asked, suddenly going into cop mode. "How low is that? Couldn't he just get a library card? They're free!"

"I can't believe the crime in this town!" Strider said. "You would think cops like you, Robin, could clean up this town better." He shot two balls into nearby pockets.

"We try!" Robin squatted down and peered over the table attempting to determine his next shot. "So, Shelly, did you catch the thieves?"

"No," I replied, amazed that my own brother was more

concerned about stolen library books than the fact that I had been followed by a creepy guy. Maybe, I should have mentioned the latter first.

Eddie, who was getting two strawberry cream sodas for the two of us, stopped mixing the pink powder in mid-stir. "Did you say someone was following you, Shelly?" he asked in a concerned voice. He came around the counter with the sodas and sat on the stool next to me.

"Finally!" I exclaimed. "Someone was actually listening," I told them what had happened to me. "I really hope the guy doesn't come around again," I said as I leaned against Eddie.

"Do you want me to bust his head for you?" Eddie asked, putting on his best Bronx accent.

"Would you?" I asked suddenly brightening up.

He nodded as he drank about half of his soda. Eddie is allergic to blood, so to compensate for his nutritional needs, he is a vegetarian. As long as he has some sort of vegetable or fruit supplement in his food and liquid intake, he is satisfied. That beats him throwing up if he accidentally digests some blood. The actual fruit content in this particular soda is suspect, though.

"Boy, Shelly, you really get the weirdos at the library," Robin replied. I gave him a full description of the stalker.

"Not every creep hangs out at the library!" I protested as I set my empty glass on the counter. "No thanks, Eddie," I said in response to his subliminal question about a refill.

"Come on," Eddie said to Robin and Strider, "Shelly does bring up a valid point. Creepy people hang out everywhere, not just at the library."

"Bus stops," Robin offered, "You can meet some pretty creepy people waiting for their bus."

"Underneath bridges are pretty creepy places as well," Strider volunteered.

Even Bruce and Dirk stopped working on the jukebox to look at the satyr. "I'm not going to even ask how you know these things, Strider," Dirk said.

"Now," I agreed, "that's just plain creepy!"

Bruce plugged in the jukebox. Suddenly, the neon lights illuminated the entire diner. "Timothy, Amelia, the jukebox is ready to go!" he shouted towards the kitchen.

My father, forty-six-year-old Timothy Anderson, came out

into the dining area with his fiancée, the lovely Amelia Cross. A smile crossed his face. "It's looking good," he replied as he and Amelia walked around to admire the piece of equipment.

"It's bright, too!" I replied as I lifted up my hands to shield my eyes from the glare. "It's bright enough to light up Vegas!"

Amelia smiled at me. "Timothy, Shelly's right. It is really bright."

"Do you think you can try to fix that light, Bruce?" Dad asked.

"I can try," Bruce said. "Here, Dirk," he told my boyfriend's brother, "let's get this thing out to Timothy's car." He unplugged the electric cord, and then they both lifted the jukebox and began carrying it to the back of the diner. The kitchen doors opened by themselves with the help of Amelia's telekinesis, and the two men lugged the object out of the diner.

"Now, there's another place where creepy people hang out, the carnival," Robin answered as he grabbed himself a cola from behind the ice cream counter. "Especially the carnies!"

"Now, that's just stereotyping, Robin," Eddie protested. "Not all carnival workers are creepy. Some are decent people!"

The tone in his voice was genuine as if he could really relate to carnies.

I looked at the vampire as I read his mind. I began laughing as he thought about the times he did mechanical work on some of the rides at different fairs. "I can't see you being a carnie, Eddie. That is so not you!"

My man shrugged. "Fine, don't believe me, babe, but you can ask your father."

I looked over at Dad who gave me an affirmative nod. "It's on his résumé," he assured me.

"Really, Eddie," I said with a smile. "So, my dad hired you because you can operate the Tilt-A-Whirl?" I teased the vampire.

"No, it was because of my great work ethic," Eddie said as he got up from his seat.

"You're probably the only carnie worker in history who wasn't strung out on drugs, Eddie," Robin replied as he pulled out his wallet from his back jean pocket. He handed Strider a twenty-dollar bill. "We've really got to stop playing pool for money," he told the satyr.

Eddie managed a grin. "Mr. Anderson, I'm going out for

lunch," he told Dad as he hopped off the barstool. He went behind the counter, took off the black apron, and stuffed it under the counter. Then he threw on the jean jacket which I had given him last Christmas and grabbed his black motorcycle helmet from under the counter. He started to head towards the back doors when I stopped him.

"Can I come with you?" I asked. I sensed something was bothering him, and he needed to talk about it.

He nodded. "Sure, babe." I followed Eddie through the kitchen and out into the parking lot. He opened the hatch on the back of his bright green motorcycle and pulled out a miniature maroon helmet that fit in the palm of his hand. He placed a hand over the helmet and murmured, "Maximum five!" Suddenly, the helmet grew to its normal size.

I took the helmet from him and pulled it over my head, snapping the latch together under my chin. I climbed on the back of the motorcycle. "So, where are we going?"

"How about that coffee shop that just opened up a few blocks away?" he suggested as he put on his helmet. Even though he is an immortal vampire, Eddie still likes to play it safe it on his motorcycle. He straddled the bike and then turned the throttle forward.

I wrapped my arms around his waist just before the motorcycle roared to life, and we sped out of the parking lot. As I leaned my head against his back, I jumped into his mind to see what was bothering him.

Eddie was jealous of his brother. The two were always on each other's nerves and at each other's necks (no pun intended) at times. Mainly, it was because of their vast differences, but this time it was different. Something had just come up and was really bothering him. I could feel the muscles in his body tense up. I stopped reading his mind. We would talk about it at the coffee shop.

The Blue Moon Café is a quaint, little hole in the wall. The cozy, green and white wallpapered restaurant can seat about twenty people. Customers can sit at the little wicker two or four-person tables, and still feel at home. Eddie and I walked up to the counter. I looked over the menu for a moment or two before deciding on a chicken Caesar wrap and a large French vanilla coffee. "Could I have two creams and four sugars in my coffee?" I asked the young elf with the various facial piercings.

He nodded and then turned to Eddie. "What about you, dude?" he asked.

"I'll have your garden salad with ranch, and a large regular coffee with cream and extra sugar."

"Sure thing, Eddie!" the teenager said.

My boyfriend wondered how this pimply-faced kid knew his name. Then he looked down and unpinned the gold plated name badge from the breast pocket of his royal blue dress shirt and shoved it into his jacket pocket. Once our food and coffee were ready to go, he reached for his wallet.

"Let me get this one," I told him as I placed a hand on his elbow. I fished the wallet from my huge black purse and handed the cashier my debit card. "Could you put both orders on debit, please?" I asked him. He rang up our purchases and handed me the receipt which I pocketed it in my khaki pants.

We grabbed our food, and we walked to a table by the window. "You didn't have to pay, Shelly," he told me.

"You always pay for our meals," I pointed out as I gingerly took a sip of my coffee. I didn't want to scald my tongue or the roof of my mouth. "Let me return the favor just this once. Don't worry about paying me back."

Eddie managed a weary grin. He tore open the packet of dressing and drizzled it all over the salad. Normally, he consumes about half of his food, but tonight he took only a few bites.

"What's wrong?" I asked him before I took a bite out of my wrap. A huge blob of mayonnaise plopped onto the table. I grabbed a napkin from the silver dispenser on the table and wiped up my mess.

"It's nothing, babe."

"You know I don't like it when you keep secrets from me."

Eddie sighed. "I'm sorry, Shelly. Just some stuff's going on."

"Like what? Your animosity towards Dirk?"

He rolled his eyes at me. Since my magical talent is more mental than physical, he often forgets that I can read his mind. He nodded. "Dirk's been getting on my nerves lately."

"Why? What's been going on?"

"You know how you've been asking me to be nice to Mr.

Miller?"

"Of course, he's your coworker and my dad's best friend!" I took another sip of my coffee. Eddie and Bruce had never gotten along since the Millers came to Zephyr from my hometown a few months ago. At first, I thought Bruce didn't like Eddie because he's a vampire, but when I saw how differently Bruce treated Dirk, I knew that was just not the case. "So, you're angry at both Dirk and Bruce, but why?"

"Where do I start? It all started when Lisa and Dirk began seriously dating. I overheard your father and Mr. Miller talking about us earlier. Mr. Miller was saying how he wished I was more like Dirk. He told your father, and I quote, 'I wish I could trust Eddie with Shelly like I trust Dirk with my Lisa!' He thinks that Dirk's better than me."

"You're nothing like your brother."

Eddie remembered his coffee and took a sip before continuing. "According to Mr. Miller, Dirk would never put Lisa in danger, like I supposedly do with you."

I laughed. "In the face of danger, your brother screams like a little girl."

Eddie laughed, too. "And what a high-pitched scream it is."

"Plus, Bruce shouldn't be worried about you putting me in danger. It's more like you're always pulling me out of danger."

"You don't think I know that!" Eddie snapped. He stabbed the fork down at a cherry tomato which bounced off his plate and onto the floor.

I set my cup down and touched his arm to calm him down. "Breathe," I told him gently.

"I'm sorry, Shelly. It's just that Mr. Miller doesn't even try to like me." He rested his head on a closed fist. The contention between Eddie and Bruce had been growing ever since my friend, Lisa, starting dating Dirk. Eddie really tries to be nice to Bruce, but he's afraid Dad would fire him if he and Bruce got into an altercation. "Mr. Miller is such a jerk."

"Eddie, just tell Dad you can't work with Bruce. Ask him to put Bruce on day shifts. Politely, of course. Dad will understand."

Eddie managed a smile. "You're right, Shell. I'll talk to your dad tonight."

Chapter Three:
The Police Lose My Stalker

The next day, I was once again shelving on the second floor when I spotted my elusive stalker. I glanced over both shoulders. The sicko was still following me. It was time to execute the perfect escape route. I glanced in the direction of the backstairs. If I took that track, I could make it to the back offices much faster. But then he might follow me down the stairs, and who knows what he would do if I suddenly become clumsy and tripped on my way down? The elevator was my second option, but I soon put that plan aside. Knowing my luck, the stupid elevator doors would open up to greet my dead body.

I decided to take the last and probably safest plan. I pretended to hear a page for me as I slowly set the books in my hands back on the cart. Then I nonchalantly walked down the huge marble staircase. A group of hyped-up, giggling kindergarten students, who were getting a tour of the building, nearly ran into me. I gave a huge sigh of relief. At least, the main stairs had lots of traffic so there was no way Uncle Creepy could try any kind of monkey business. I picked up the pace a bit and speed-walked the rest of the way.

"Raquel!" I hissed to the werewolf. Then I realized she was on the phone at the front desk. That guy was following me again. I glanced over my shoulder as I sent her the urgent telepathic message. Short, fat, and creepy had seated himself at one of the computers, and was, surprise, surprise, still staring at me.

Shelly, call the police, Raquel told me.

I casually picked up an available phone, and after a couple of minutes, I finally figured out how to dial 911. I never had to call the police before while I was at work and was unsure if there was a special method for calling them. Finally, I got through and told the dispatcher what the problem was after she took me off hold. It is always comforting to know that the police are so busy they have to put someone on hold.

Two uniformed rookie officers met with me at the front desk. After I gave them the Readers' Digest condensed version of what had happened, the elf and the fairy arrested the guy. The taller of the two, the fairy, flew over on her black and yellow butterfly wings and placed a hand on the man's shoulder. "Sir," she said, "we need to have a word with you downtown!"

He got up reluctantly and was about to be led away by the two officers when he turned to face me. His face twisted into an evil smile. Then his mouth started moving.

Suddenly a bright light flashed before my eyes as if the lights had flickered. I stared blankly into space for a moment or two. It was as if someone had stolen a piece of me or something. I shook myself out of the weird trance and went back to work. I was relieved that my stalker was not going to be bothering me again.

I was sitting in the staff room taking my afternoon break when I heard the volunteer paging me over the intercom. "Shelly, you have a phone call on 7328!" I took another bite out of the chocolate bar, pried myself from the comfort of the ugly, but cozy pink leather couch and walked over to the phone.

I knew it wasn't Eddie because he doesn't wake up until

after three. Plus, he would call my cell phone. "This is Shelly," I said after dialing the extension.

"Shelly, it's Robin," my brother hesitated as he spoke. "I've got some good news and bad news."

"Well, what's the good news?" I asked, uncertain as to why he called.

"Brooke is coming to visit tomorrow."

"Oh, that's cool!" I said. I was the one who had inadvertently brought Robin and Brooke together just a few months before. He had been dating her long-distance since she lived over two hours away. This was the first time that Brooke would be coming to visit Zephyr. "Where's she staying?"

"She's staying with some relatives."

"Is she going to meet Dad and Amelia?"

"Definitely!"

Then I realized this conversation wasn't probably the real reason Robin had called. "So, what's the bad news?"

My brother hesitated. "Well, the guy who was following you seems to have disappeared."

"What!" I nearly yelled into the receiver. Fortunately, I was the only one in the staff room.

"Ow! Ow!" Robin said. "That was my ear! Look, don't blame me. The two officers told me that when they were transporting him to the station for questioning, he said some kind of magical spell and disappeared. They apparently didn't use the proper handcuffs."

"They didn't use magical-restraining handcuffs on him? What were they thinking?" I yelled for the second time in less than thirty seconds.

"Come on, Shell, give them a break. They're just rookies."

"Yeah, rookies who have let a potentially dangerous man on the loose."

"Look, you said he doesn't know you. So, you should be all set."

"Gee, thanks!" I said with an unappreciated eye-roll.

"If you see him again, just call us, and we'll arrest him. My pager's going off! I'll talk to you later, bye!"

"Okay, bye." I hung up the phone and slumped back to my seat where my candy bar awaited me. Chocolate is usually an antidepressant for me, but when I took another bite, it suddenly didn't taste so good anymore. This was going to be a long

afternoon.

Chapter Four

Jordan is Put into the Animal Hospital

When I went out to the grazing lot, I knew that something was wrong. In case you're wondering what a grazing lot is, you have to know something about the transportation methods here in Zephyr. Cars and motorcycles are considered luxuries. Most people ride unicorns, dragons, winged horses, and other strange creatures. Almost every building has a grazing lot equipped with a large barn to shield the animals from the elements. I walked over to the post where I had tied my winged horse, Jordan, and noticed the blood oozing down one of her chocolate brown wings. "Hey, what happened to you?" I asked her as I gently touched her wing. She gave an anguished whinny. Normally, I tie my canvas bag to her saddle strings, but I decided against it. Instead, I stuffed my purse inside the bag and swung it over my shoulder. Then I untied the reins from the post and walked alongside her out of the lot.

Instead of flying, I walked beside her to the animal hospital which was only a block away. I tied her to an available post and went inside the large office building. The nymph sitting at the desk looked up at me with her big, dark blue eyes. "May I help you?" she asked me.

I nodded. "Is Doctor Montogmery in today?" I asked.

She nodded. "Yes!"

"I'm Shelly Anderson, and I was wondering if she could take a look at Jordan. One of her wings seems to be broken or something." She handed me a clipboard with a form to fill out and brushed my hand with her long, red nails.

I sat down on one of the charcoal gray cushioned chairs and began filling out some paperwork about what happened to Jordan. After I handed back the form, I glanced around the office as the receptionist walked out to the back office. Dr. Beth Montgomery always keeps a community bulletin board up in the waiting room. As I glanced over the various advertisements of houses for sale, free puppies, and neighborhood potluck suppers, I spotted a bright pink poster. In huge block lettering, it read: Get Ready for the 650th Annual Summer Moon Festival!

"That sounds fun," I said to myself as I sat back down on the chair. I picked up some celebrity magazine and flipped through it, not really paying attention. The fair was starting tomorrow night, and this was really great timing because my boyfriend was starting his week-long vacation tonight. Maybe I'll suggest to Eddie about going to the carnival when I see him tonight.

"Shelly Anderson?"

I put the magazine down and got up to greet the plump, gray-haired Welkie dressed in green scrubs. Welkies are a race of humans who possess all kinds of magical powers. They are better known as wizards, sorcerers, witches, and enchantresses. "Hello, Dr. Montogmery," I said as I shook the enchantress' hand.

"Hello, Shelly. You said that Jordan's been having trouble with her wings."

I nodded.

"Well, let's go take a look."

I had the receptionist hold my canvas bag and purse behind her desk. Then I showed the enchantress out to the parking lot. I grimaced as she lifted up the wing of the horse.

There was a long silence as the veterinarian examined Jordan.

"So, how long has her wing been broken?"

I shrugged. "It was fine this morning. She didn't seem to be in any pain when we flew this morning. But I noticed her wing was bleeding just before I came here."

Dr. Montgomery shook her head sadly. "Unfortunately, her wing has been broken in two places." She gently untied Jordan's reins and began leading her to the back of the office where a large green barn stood. She opened up the door of an empty stall, and Jordan slowly went inside. "I'll look at her right away, but I won't be able to tell you anything until sometime next week."

"Thanks, Dr. Montgomery," I told her as we walked into the office through a back door. "I really appreciate you seeing Jordan so quickly."

She smiled at me. "It was my pleasure, Shelly!" She must have realized that I didn't have any way to get home because she asked if I needed a ride.

"No, thanks," I replied. "My boyfriend can pick me up," I

said goodbye and got my canvas bag from the receptionist. I could barely get cell phone service here so I stepped outside in the cool air, watching the setting sun. Splashes of orange and purple rays painted the blue sky. The one thing that I like about Zephyr is no matter what time of the year it is, the sun always sets around six o'clock. And the sunsets are always beautiful. Unfortunately, the only way that vampires, like Eddie, can enjoy them is by looking through UV-protected glass. I sat on a small patch of grass and dialed Eddie's cell number.

He picked up on the third ring. "Y'llo?"

"Are you busy right now, Eddie?" I asked him.

"Well, I was half-way through my shower when you called."

The very thought of my dripping wet boyfriend in a towel wrapped around his waist sent a delightful shiver up my spine. *No naughty thoughts*, Shelly, I scolded myself. Then I remembered he was still on the line. "Can you pick me up at Dr. Montgomery's? One of Jordan's wings is broken, and she doesn't know how long it will take to heal."

"Sure, babe! I'll be there in about a half-hour."

"Love you," I said. I closed my phone and drew my knees close to my chest. Poor Jordan. I hated seeing her in pain. Even though she was a winged horse, she meant a lot to me. How on earth did her wing break? What would happen to her? I brushed away the tears.

Stop worrying, Shelly! I could almost hear Eddie's voice echoing in my head. My telepathy only works when the undead are in the same room as me, so I knew that my boyfriend wasn't around.

My stomach growled. By the time Eddie got here, it would be almost seven. I dug around my canvas bag and pulled out a small bag of chips. I slowly ate them. Fortunately, they weren't going to be my supper. It was Thursday, and Eddie and I had developed a weekly ritual of pizza and a movie at his house. My boyfriend wouldn't like it if I ruined my appetite. I opened up the murder mystery in hopes of getting past the first twenty pages.

I was so engrossed in my book that I almost missed the honk of a car horn. Eddie was sitting at the wheel of one of his homemade cars. This particular car is in the shape of a carrot, which he uses whenever he races. I gathered up my bag and purse and hurried over to the car. After I threw the bag behind the passenger seat, I opened the passenger door and slid into the seat.

"Hey," Eddie said with a furrowed brow, "why didn't you tell me your stalker escaped from the police? Robin called to tell me about it."

I pulled the seat belt across my lap and snapped it shut. "Sorry," I said softly. "I'm just worried about Jordan."

He gave my hand a gentle squeeze. It was good to know he wasn't mad at me but concerned for my safety. "So, what happened to her?"

I shrugged. "I don't know. When I got out to the grazing lot, I noticed one of Jordan's wings was injured. My main concern was to get her to the animal hospital." Then a horrifying thought crossed my mind. I gave a sharp gasp. "What if that guy was the one who hurt her?"

"Your stalker?"

I nodded as I remembered what had happened when the guy was being led away by the police. "Something else weird happened to me. That guy said something to me, and it felt like something was taken away from my memory."

A shocked look appeared on Eddie's face. Before he became a vampire, my boyfriend used to be a wizard. He still retains some of his magical spells. From reading his mind, I found out the creep had used some kind of spell on me. "He put a very basic memory reading spell on you," Eddie explained in answer to my puzzled look. He pulled the car out of the parking lot. "The spell allows the Welkie to have access to your basic memory. It's like someone looking at your license. This guy knows your name, where you live, and what kind of animal you ride. He probably was the one who broke Jordan's wing."

"Great! Just what I need." I looked out the window at all the houses and businesses we drove past. No creepy guy was following us. I had so much on my mind right now with a creepy man casting spells on me and Jordan's broken wing.

I was about to ask Eddie to swing by my house so I could drop off my bag when I remembered Lisa and Dirk were having dinner there. Lisa Miller, my best friend from high school and my current roommate, had just gotten back from some kind of wedding planners' conference only the night before and was having Dirk over for dinner at my place. "So, are we going to pick up the pizza before or after we get a movie?" I asked.

"I think there's a frozen pizza at the house," Eddie replied as he turned on his left blinker. "We might as well just pick up a movie and head over to my place." He sounded a bit unsure about me coming over. Instead, he suddenly changed the subject. "I'm curious," he said as we waited for the longest light on the face of the planet to turn green. "How did the police lose this guy?"

"Robin said they forgot to put on magical restraining handcuffs. The officers were rookies!"

"No offense to your brother, but that news just decreased my confidence in the Zephyr police force."

"Tell me about it!" We pulled into The Movie Palace and walked inside. After a fifteen-minute debate on whether we should get a comedy or an action movie (we finally chose the comedy), we headed back to the Van Helsing mansion.

Eddie pulled the car into the large garage attached to the

green house he shares with his brother and sister. He immediately noticed the opened door leading into the kitchen. "Does he think we live in a barn?" he grumbled. He maneuvered the car in between a beat-up, pickle-shaped car and a car in the shape of a zucchini. The moment we opened the car doors, we were both hit with the smell of griffin manure, which has the distinct smell of moldy potatoes.

"When did you guys get a griffin?" I asked waving my hand in front of my face in a futile attempt to combat the awful stench.

"Since Luken got here last week," Eddie said as he gingerly stepped over the steaming pile of griffin turd. Even though these creatures are truly magnificent with the heads, feet, and wings of an eagle and the body of a lion, they can leave quite a stinky impression.

I noticed in the back of the garage a new stall had been built right next to where Dirk's dragon, Ringo, sleeps. A tan griffin was plucking out its feathers. I now realized why Eddie prefers cars and motorcycles over smelly animals. Plugging our noses, we sprinted into the kitchen, slamming the door behind us. "So, when did your cousin and his smelly griffin get here?" I asked

Eddie.

Eddie opened the freezer door and pulled out a

medium-size frozen cheese pizza. "Last week," he said in a

disgruntled tone. Apparently, Luken had been giving him a lot of

grief lately. Eddie realized I was reading his mind again. "He's

been a pain in the butt ever since he arrived here!"

I was about to ask why when I noticed a leopard-skin

purse sitting on the kitchen table. "Whose purse is that?" I knew

it didn't belong to Eddie's sister, Fern. For one thing, she's a

ghost and has no need for a purse.

"Probably one of Luken's lady friends left it here."

"Oh, does he have many of those?"

Eddie nodded. "You can call them 'lady friends with

benefits.'" That was the reason why he hadn't invited me over at

all this week. Much to Eddie's disapproval, Luken had been

enjoying Zephyr's various escort services.

"Well, I'll go set up the movie!" I said as I grabbed the

case from under the vampire's arm. I headed towards the living

room, not really noticing the noises from the couch. I thought that someone must have left the television on. "Eddie," I called back as I entered the living room, "we should make some popcorn, too—What the!" I shrieked.

What should have been my first clue was the clothing thrown about the living room. Two blond heads popped up from behind the couch. The first vampire's face was smeared with an amazing array of make-up and her blond hair was teased with probably three cans of hairspray. The guy vampire, whom I deduced was Luken, had a completely unfazed look on his pretty-boy face. "Dude, do you need anything?" he drawled.

I slowly placed one foot behind the other, trying to retreat with dignity. "Um—no. I don't need anything. Ah, I'm just going to, ah, leave. Carry on!" I said, waving my hand around with a failed attempt at nonchalance. Thank God, the only thing I saw were their faces.

I sprinted back to the kitchen. "Um, Eddie,—I don't know how to word this, but—."

"Word what?" Eddie asked cautiously as he retrieved two sodas from the fridge. "Why?"

"I have just decided I'm never going to sit on your sofa

again. Or maybe anything else here."

"What? Why won't you sit on the couch?"

"Well, your cousin is certainly getting his money's worth on your couch right now."

"Money's worth? Wait-is he with some woman?"

"Yes, they're doing the nasty on your couch. I could only see their faces, thankfully."

Eddie's face was slowly becoming a quite alarming shade of purple. "He's with a woman right now? In my house? On my couch?" he roared.

"Um—yeah—I mean—I wouldn't have mentioned it, but it was rather shocking since it was quite unexpected." Eddie's temper was rising, and I was becoming startled at his reaction to my tale.

"Well, I'm going to stop it right now! I'm not going to harbor his disgusting habits here!" Eddie exclaimed. He barreled into the adjoining room, me following hesitantly, torn between curiosity and dread. Entering the room, I found the situation exactly as I had found it before.

"Just what do you think you're doing?" Eddie growled

between clenched teeth.

Luken's head popped up again. "What do you mean, 'what do you think I'm doing?'"

I held back a snort of laughter that had risen with the comical response.

Eddie was choking on his words, not from laughter though. "If you don't leave right now, I will not be responsible for my actions."

"Well, Eddie, I believe you are being unspeakably rude." Then he noticed me. "Who is this pretty lady, may I ask?"

"None of your business," Eddie growled. "Leave the house. Now. Come back without your friend or don't come back at all."

"Oh, you're rather hypocritical. You have a lady friend over, too, my dear cousin."

"Shelly is my girlfriend," Eddie snarled.

"All right, all right. I'll go," Luken said, completely oblivious to how dangerously low Eddie's voice had become. "But I really don't see what the problem is. I do respect you though, so I'll be going. You might want to go into the kitchen so we can get dressed in private. Bunny here is very modest."

Wow, Luken was pretty and dumb! The stereotypes live on!

Another snort of laughter threatened to resurface, and I repressed it with much difficulty. I hurried back into the kitchen and began laughing hysterically. But when my boyfriend entered the room, it quickly became a tactful coughing fit. Being in the same house with the two vampires was probably not the safest thing for anyone right at the moment. I suddenly had an epiphany: the perfect distraction. "Eddie, I still haven't bought a gift for Amelia's bridal shower. Why don't we skip the movie and head over to the mall right now?"

Chapter Five:

I Learn a Bit More about My Stalker

The car ride to the mall was pretty quiet. Eddie's hands were gripping the steering wheel as he silently devised various ways to kill his cousin and make it look like an accident. Finally, he spoke, "So, you still haven't gotten Amelia a bridal shower gift?"

I shook my head. "I just don't know what to get her. I mean, this is her second wedding. So, what would you get someone who's been married once already?"

Eddie shrugged. "I don't know. I've never been to a bridal shower." He pulled the car into an available space at the end of the Moonlight Mall parking lot. We walked hand-in-hand to the twenty-four-hour mall entrance. The vampire had cooled off and was now smiling, but I could sense he wanted to talk.

My stomach was growling loudly, and I felt like I was going to faint from hunger. The minute we walked into the mall, I dragged the Eddie over to the little pizzeria in the food court. "Do you want to split a personal pan cheese pizza?" I asked.

"Sure," he replied. "But this time, let me pay!" He smiled at me as he fished out his wallet from the back of his jeans. We told the satyr behind the counter we wanted a small cheese pizza, and the satyr gave us two empty medium-sized Styrofoam cups. Eddie got himself a diet iced tea from the soda fountain while I decided to be naughty and went for a high-calorie, sugar-filled neon green drink. Then we sat down at an available table for two. Eddie was eyeing my soda warily. "You're going to be up all night with that in your system!"

I smirked. "So, what! At least, it tastes sweet."

"My diet iced tea is healthy."

"So, your iced tea is going to balance out the six-hundred calorie pizza we're having?"

Eddie had to think about my revelation for a moment. Then he smiled at me. "Why do your crazy ideas always make sense to me?"

"Because you're blinded by your love?" I said with a huge smile. Then I started giggling when I remembered the humorous confrontation with his cousin. "Speaking of love, your cousin seemed to be in some sort of love with that woman!"

Eddie rolled his eyes at me. "Luken is a perverted

mooch!"

"No, Eddie, tell me how you really feel."

"Not funny," he growled.

I held up my hands in surrender. "I was just joking!"

Eddie rarely got angry. Other than with Luken, the only time I have seen his anger was with his college roommate. He softened his voice as not to scare me. "Sorry, babe," he said. "Luken has been getting on my nerves lately."

"I came to that conclusion when you nearly ripped his head off earlier."

"It's just he has broken almost every rule Dirk and I have set!"

"Like what?"

Eddie was about to answer when our order number was called. He got up and grabbed the food. He set the pizza box down on the wrought iron table with an aggravated thud! He slumped down in his seat and dealt out a piece for each of us. Finally, he answered my question. "Dirk and I told him if he was going to stay with us, he would have to follow some rules, such as clean up after himself, and help with the groceries, that sort of stuff. I also told him under no circumstances could he have sex with women in the house. If he wants to do it in a hotel room, that's his business. Luken is a pig! My computer crashed because it got a virus from one of the porn sites he downloaded. And Dirk is not helping at all." His pizza was cooling off, and he finally took a huge bite of it.

I let him chew his food before I asked my next question. "What has Dirk got to do with this?"

"It's like he doesn't care that Luken's breaking the rules. Both Dirk and Lisa have said I'm too strict with Luken. Sometimes, I think that I'm the only adult there!" Eddie's hands were waving frantically in absolute agitation. There was no way to prevent his glass from tipping over. The iced tea flowed across the table, under my plate, and onto my clean jeans. The look on his face changed from anger to one of apology. "I'm so sorry, babe," he said as he quickly pushed back his chair and came over to my side. He grabbed a pile of napkins from the table dispenser.

"It's all right, Eddie," I said as I took the napkins from him and began to wipe at the huge, wet spot on my jeans. Like any other cheap, bulk napkins, these had no absorbency whatsoever. It looked like I had just peed my pants. Out of the corner of my eye, I saw the unmistakable white and red trucker's hat and the black trench coat. "Holy crap!" I said under my breath as I slid under the table.

Eddie's head of curly hair peered under the table. "What are you doing, Shelly?"

"That's him!" I hissed. I pointed to the guy who stood in front of a toy shop window. His creepiness had risen another notch. "That's the guy who was stalking me!"

Eddie glanced over at him and then looked under the table again. "Are you sure?" Even though the vampire is willing to protect me at any cost, he didn't want to jump to any conclusions.

I nodded vigorously. "Do something! Make me invisible!" I desperately pleaded in a low voice.

"I can only do a handful of spells, and an invisibility spell isn't one of them." A stale French fry crunched under his knees as he knelt down beside me.

I peered cautiously over the tabletop. Everyone around us

was staring at the crazy couple hiding under the table. My stalker had made eye contact with me and began walking towards me, but suddenly he stopped in his tracks when Eddie rose to his feet. This vampire is no heavy-weight champion, but he is twice as strong as the average guy on the street. The man turned on his heel and hurried away. With Eddie's outstretched hand, I pulled myself to my feet and sat back down. "Is he really gone?" He nodded as he tried to remember where he had seen my stalker before. Suddenly, it came to him. "That's Ahab Boko!" he exclaimed.

"Who?" I asked.

"Ahab Boko is a Welkie who had skipped bail back when I was a fugitive apprehension agent."

"What did he do?" This guy must have done something horrible for my boyfriend to remember him.

Eddie saw the look of alarm on my face. "No, he didn't kill anyone! He was just a little kooky! His magic practicing was put on probation several weeks before his incident with the kids. The Wixom Merlin Lodge had revoked his membership after he put curses on lodge members who he didn't like. He was arrested after he sent two gargoyles after the vice president of the lodge's grandchildren."

I shuddered involuntarily when the vampire mentioned gargoyles. My back still has the scars that one of those vicious stone creatures gave me about six months ago. "Were the kids harmed?"

Eddie shook his head. "No, just scared." He remembered my incident with the gargoyles because he was the one who saved my life. He gave my hand a gentle squeeze. "Boko skipped bail, and he was my fugitive."

"Did you catch him?"

Eddie shook his head again as he took a bite out of his pizza slice. "No, he disappeared altogether. Nobody could find him. After a while the case was dropped, and he was presumed dead."

I swallowed hard. Could this day get any worse? My stalker turned out to be a kooky, but very dangerous sorcerer on the lam. My winged horse was in the animal hospital with a broken wing. My boyfriend was contemplating killing his cousin. Speaking of which. "So, what are you going to do about Luken, aside from killing him and making it look like an accident?" I asked.

Eddie shrugged as he took a sip of my drink which I offered him. "I don't know, Shelly. His mother is Aunt Phoebe's closest sister, and you know how I feel about ruining relationships."

"You want my opinion?"

"Sure."

"Kick your perverted, moocher cousin to the curb. Thank God, you're not blood-related to him. Don't take no for an answer, not even from Dirk. Tell Luken his actions tonight have permanently scarred me for life."

"Really?"

"Believe me, it will take years and years of therapy to scrub that scene from my mind."

He grinned at me as the wheels in his head began to turn. "I can also threaten to have him arrested for solicitation!"

"It'll be less messy than the 'accidental death' thing you were planning." After a slight pause, I added as an afterthought. "And burn that couch."

"I'll definitely do it," Eddie promised. "You're the best, babe." He reached over and held both of my hands.

For a couple of minutes or so, we looked into each other's eyes. I had been dating Eddie for almost six months, but each moment I was with him, my love grew stronger. What a lucky girl I am, I told myself. Then I remembered the wet spot on my jeans which ruined the Kodak moment. "First, I really need to get a new pair of jeans, and we can go shopping for Amelia's gift."

Chapter Six:
I Find the Perfect Gift

After we dumped our empty cups and the pizza box in the trash can, I made a beeline for Merlot's, an inexpensive clothing store, and in my haste, I didn't see the sign advertising a local artisan display in the tiny boutique.

I rummaged through the first rack, attempting to find a cheap pair of jeans my size when Eddie held up a pair of Barney the Dinosaur purple jeans with green swirly things on them. "Absolutely not!" I told him.

"Sorry," he said, "but that's the only size they have."

I shook my head and pointed to my shirt. "I'm wearing an orange shirt. And do you realize how badly those two colors are going to clash?"

Eddie put the pants back on the clothes rack and

continued looking. "Oh, I forgot to tell you," he said to me. "I talked to your dad, and you were right. He completely understood."

"See, I told you he would. To think you doubted me!" I reached for a dark blue pair, but once I learned they were too small, I had to put them back. Almost all of the good jeans had been sold already.

Eddie was about to mention something else when we both heard, "Shelly, what are you doing here?"

I heard my friend's voice and grabbed the ugly pants off the rack. "Shopping," I said hurriedly as I used the pants to shield the huge pseudo-urine stain.

My best friend from childhood looked at me with her green eyes. "Really?" Lisa Miller asked as she brushed back a piece of the bleach blonde hair that had fallen out of her French braid. Then she saw the pants that I was holding. "Those pants are adorable! Aren't they, Dirk?" she asked her boyfriend. "It's so great how stores promote our artists."

Dirk shrugged. "I guess so," he replied. Anything to please Lisa.

I glanced over at Eddie who was shocked that Lisa was serious. He had shown me the pants only as a joke. Those pants are hideous, he telecommunicated to me.

Tell me about it! I returned. I glanced at the price tag. Sixty-five druci for these ugly things! But considering the fact that I didn't want the whole world to think I had no bladder control, I was going to have to buy them. But it would be a cold day in Hell before I would combine these pants with the orange shirt I was wearing. Sensing my desperation, Eddie suggested that we look at the selection of skirts. I glanced closely at the objects lining the hem of a skirt. Are those pocket watches? And who would decorate the front pockets with cotton swabs? I hurriedly flipped the skirt around to see what atrocities adored the back. Thankfully, nothing.

I quickly found a pair of capris lined with sheep's wool. I glanced over at Eddie. He was thinking the same thing I was: Isn't the point of capris to lower your body temperature? I pulled a black t-shirt from a nearby table. *Black matches anything*, I told myself. I returned the Capri's back to where I had found them, and reluctantly decided to try on the ugly, purple jeans.

"Well, I'm going to try these on!" I said clutching the clothing to cover my spot. I nearly sprinted to the fitting rooms and darted into an available stall. Drawing the curtain close, I glanced at myself in the full-length mirror. The spot on my jeans was huge! I changed out of them and slipped into the ugly pants. "Oh, crap!" I said aloud.

"What, they don't fit?" Lisa asked me. She had apparently followed me and was standing outside the fitting room.

"No, they fit perfectly!" I replied. *That's the problem,* I told myself. I pulled the black t-shirt over my head. "So, how was dinner?"

"We ordered out. I thought you and Eddie were going to be at his place?"

"No, I stumbled upon his cousin in their living room." I decided to get Eddie's opinion on the outfit. Even with the cute black shirt, I knew what his opinion would be. I turned around to see if there was any way to make the jeans likable. I guess black doesn't match everything.

"Oh, Luken seems like a nice guy,"

"Yeah, he and some lady were making out on the couch."

"Oh, Dirk and I make out there all the time," Lisa said in a blasé tone. When I pulled back the curtain and stepped out of the room, she beamed at me. "Oh, Shelly, you look so cute!"

I nodded my thanks and continued with the gossip. "I'm not talking about kissing. I'm talking about—What's an appropriate term? Doing the nasty?"

"On the couch!" Lisa asked in absolute horror. "Eew! Did they cover the couch at least?"

I shook my head. "Nope, I don't believe anything was covered, but don't worry. Luken insists Bunny is very modest! Suffice it to say, Eddie was not a happy camper."

"Riiight! I'm never going to look at that couch the same way again."

"Don't worry. I advised Eddie to burn it."

We headed back to the storefront where our boyfriends were having a fairly heated conversation.

"It's my house, Eddie. I own it, in case you forgot," Dirk snapped. "And I say Luken can do what he wants. He's an adult."

"That adult is turning the house into a brothel, which is

illegal, the last time I checked," his brother retorted.

"He's family. We can't just kick him out."

"We can certainly try." They immediately stopped talking about their cousin the moment they saw us. Eddie literally jumped back a foot or more. He stumbled over his words. "You look—um—pretty? I don't think the pants bring out your eyes, babe," he said cautiously.

"Pants bring out your eyes?" Lisa murmured to herself, but let it pass.

"Ooh," I said pointing to a pair of Bermuda shorts. The dark green shorts looked less daunting with only one orange streak blazing down the sides. The price was three times cheaper than its hideous brother. "And," I said, "they match my orange shirt."

Dirk looked at Eddie. "The green will bring out her blue eyes," he said, cocking an eyebrow ironically. Dirk is smarter than he looks.

"I'll be right back!" I darted back into the stall and quickly tried on the shorts. "They don't look that bad," I said out loud. "I mean, I wouldn't give them to my worst enemy." I changed back into my old jeans. As I walked out, I held the shorts in front of me with the Barney jeans in my hand as if they possessed a pungent smell. "I'm getting the shorts."

Lisa let out a little groan. "But the jeans are so cute."

"I don't have anything to match them," I lied.

"Are you sure the shorts aren't a little too gaudy or flamboyant?"

"Nope, I think they look great and kind of sporty."

The guys seemed to be bemused at our conversation. "Real sporty," Eddie replied with just a hint of sarcasm.

"Super-duper sporty," Dirk added.

"Thank you," I said through gritted teeth. I paid for my merchandise and quickly walked to a nearby bathroom where I change into the "sporty" shorts with lightning speed. When I walked out to the bench where Eddie, Dirk, and Lisa were waiting for me, I showed off the shorts. "What do you think?"

I think I need to take a fork to my eyeballs in order to blot this image from my mind, Eddie thought, but wisely said nothing. He gave a polite cough which masked the word "disgusting."

Lisa and Dirk didn't say anything about my flamboyant

outfit. "Dirk and I have to get going so that we can buy decorations for Amelia's bridal shower," Lisa said.

"Oh, that's what Shelly and I are doing here," Eddie blurted out before I could stop him. "Shelly hasn't bought her a gift yet." I shot him a dirty look which ceased his incessant babbling.

"You haven't bought her a gift, Shelly!" Lisa exclaimed in shock. "It's this Sunday! You have known about this for two months."

I stammered for an explanation, but nothing came to my mind. I didn't really want to tell her the truth which was I had no idea what to get for Amelia. Lisa was planning Dad and Amelia's wedding, and with her personality, she doesn't like it when things aren't in her control.

Lisa gave an exaggerated sigh. "Oh, well! Come on, Dirk. Shelly, see you tonight!" She and Dirk waved good-bye to us and walked off.

Once we were left alone, Eddie took another look at my outfit. He shook his head sadly. "May I say I never want to see you in those shorts again, Shelly?"

"Don't worry, Eddie. I'm planning on burning them when I get home! Could you carry the bag for me? It has my pants in it."

Eddie took the plastic bag from me and swung it over his shoulder. "Oh, by the way, I wanted to tell you something. When I talked to your dad, he promoted me. Once I get back from vacation, I'll be a night manager at the diner."

I beamed with joy. "Congratulations!" I gave him our standard high-five. "That's so awesome, Eddie."

Eddie smiled for a moment, and then he frowned when he thought about the recent conversation with Lisa. "Why did you give me that dirty look when I told Lisa you hadn't picked out a gift?"

I dug my hands into my pockets as we walked into a huge department store. "I didn't want her to know I have no idea what to get Amelia. You know how Lisa is. Everything has to go according to schedule or else the planets will collide and cause the end of the world. Plus, Lisa already bought Amelia an expensive silver tea set. So, anything I get will seem cheap!"

Eddie put an arm around me. "Shelly, I know this is going to sound really corny, but there's really no other way to say it.

Amelia will love whatever you get for her." He kissed the top of my head.

"You're right, hon," I told him I really needed to focus on buying my future stepmother a gift from my heart. "And that speech was really corny. Actually, I have been thinking that maybe you and I should go in on the actual wedding gift together because we're a couple and everything."

"Let me guess! You don't know what to get them for the wedding."

"Let's just concentrate on the bridal shower gift. I'm not even going to worry about their wedding gift now. We'll cross that bridge when we come to it." We headed in the general direction of the women's department. Maybe I could buy Amelia a nice dress or something. I smacked my forehead with the palm of my hand. Come on, Shelly, you can do better than that. "What do you think I should get Amelia?" I asked him.

"What about some lingerie?" Eddie suggested. "Don't women always give that stuff at bridal showers?"

I looked at him. "You're not serious, are you? She's going to be my stepmother. What am I going to say on the card? 'Hope this gets my dad in the mood?' "

Eddie blushed as he considered how awkward the situation would be. "Point taken. What about a picture frame?"

"That's a cop-out gift for someone you really don't know." Boy, Eddie was not helping at all. We walked into the cosmetics department. I thought about buying Amelia perfume but decided against it when I realized I had no idea what scent she wore.

I began staring at all the sparkling jewelry under the glass counters. "Ooh! This one is pretty," I said as I pointed to a pretty, turquoise stone trio on a petite silver chain.

Eddie looked at the necklace. "That's really beautiful." He motioned to the fairy wiping off the glass of the counter. "Could we see this turquoise necklace, please?"

The clerk unlocked the case. "You, my friend, have chosen a very popular item among the ladies," he told my boyfriend in a very eager tone. He carefully took the necklace in his hand as if it were a fragile piece of glass. He sucked in his breath as Eddie took the necklace from him.

My boyfriend lifted up my ponytail with one hand and then draped the necklace around my neck. After putting my hair in front of my shoulder, he fastened the clasp. "What do you think?" he asked when the clerk handed me a small mirror.

Even though Eddie has no reflection, I could sense him smiling at me. The instant I saw the necklace, I fell in love with it. "Wow!" I said in awe. If I wasn't trying to find a present for Amelia, I would've definitely added this to my small jewelry collection. Then, I looked at the price tag. It was way out of my price range.

"Let me see!" Eddie said. When I turned around, he gave a low whistle. "Wow! That is really stunning on you, Shelly!"

"That is truly your color, miss," the clerk said.

"Do you think that Amelia will like it?" I asked Eddie.

"What?" he asked. He was thinking that the necklace was for me, not Amelia. "I don't know, babe. It's kind of pricey, don't you think?"

I nodded reluctantly. Eddie was right, plus, my dad was always giving Amelia jewelry anyway. "You're right," I sighed as I unhooked the clasp. I hesitantly gave the necklace back to the clerk, not wanting to let it go.

I felt like giving up. There was absolutely nothing to get

Amelia. I felt like a heel until I saw the perfect gift. Sitting on a shelf was a soft pink jewelry box with two glass doors on the top and six tiny pull-out drawers with adorable brass knobs in the shapes of roses. I pulled out a drawer and ran my finger along the soft black velvet lining. Everything about this jewelry box was perfect, including the discounted price. Even Eddie agreed with me.

Eddie took me back to his place later that evening. Luken's griffin was gone, but the pile of turd was still sitting in the garage. As soon as he parked the car, the vampire sprinted inside the house, leaving me in the garage. When he came back, he tossed a set of keys to me. "While Jordan's out of commission, you can use the picklemobile."

"Thanks, Eddie," I said as I set my purse and the two bags in the passenger seat of the picklemobile. This car is green, ugly, and in the shape of a pickle. Eddie has had this car for about thirty years and has always has spent way too much money for repairs. He only keeps it around for sentimental reasons. "Hey," I asked, remembering the poster at the vet's office, "do you want to go to the fair tomorrow night?"

"Sure, I'd love to, Shelly," he said as he reached into the back pocket of his jeans and pulled out a tiny black bag. Using a maximizing spell, he increased the bag to the size of a briefcase. Then he opened up the bag he used when he was a spy and a bounty hunter. He laid it flat on the hood of the car. After shuffling through wooden stakes, silver throwing stars, he pulled out a high-powered pistol and a cartridge of laser bullets. "I want you to have these in case that Boko guy tries to harm you. And this." He handed me the pistol and the bullets, along with a stun gun. "I'll see you tomorrow night at seven. Have a good night, babe," he said as he planted a warm kiss on my lips.

I returned the kiss. It took me a few minutes to pull away from him, mainly because I didn't want to. "See you later," I said in a soft voice as I slid behind the steering wheel. I set both guns and the bullets onto the passenger seat

"Bye, Shelly!" Eddie called as he walked back inside his house. He hit the garage door opener that was attached to the garage's wall and waved good-bye to me.

"Bye, Eddie!" I turned on the engine and put the car in

reverse. It sputtered a little, but finally, it roared or shall I say, coughed, to life. "Please, don't let this thing die on me," I pleaded to the car gods. I made it home safely with no sign of my stalker and no sign of the engine or some other important piece of the car falling out alongside the road.

Chapter Seven:
I'm On Top of the World

The smell of cotton candy and doughboys wafted through the air as Eddie and I walked from the parking lot to the Zephyr Summer Moon Fairgrounds. Even though the moon was almost at full peak, the fluorescent lights lit up the night sky. Eddie was wearing a red and blue striped polo shirt that had fallen over the waistline of his jean shorts. "I noticed that you're not wearing those god awful shorts, Shelly!"

I looked down at my grey cropped pants and light pink t-shirt. "I know. I tossed them in the trash the second I got home," I said with a laugh. I reached into my pants pockets for my money. My purse was too bulky to carry around, so I left it in the vampire's car. I glanced up at the entrance gate sign. Adults: $12.50. "Is it me or has the admission tickets gone up this year?"

"It was only five druci last year," Eddie replied as he pulled out some cash. Experience had taught him to never use credit cards at carnivals.

An old centaur standing behind the booth quickly slid the girly magazine he was reading under a pile of papers. "You want to buy a five-day wristband for three druci more?" he asked. Eddie and I looked at each other. We really were only going to spend a few hours here. One can take the carnie atmosphere for only so long. "No, thanks," I said. "We're just going to get two passes for tonight."

Both Eddie and I handed the guy our money. After the centaur rang up it up on a cheap cash register, two purple plastic wristbands spewed out of a black machine the size of a shoebox. We were given tickets, and the worker unlocked the turnstile. Once we were inside, I immediately spotted my brother and his girlfriend waiting inside for us. "Hey, guys!" I called as I waved to them.

Brooke Luptin greeted me warmly with a huge hug. "Hey, Shelly. Haven't seen you in a while," the half-elf, half-enchantress said with a twinkle in her indigo blue eyes. A blue do-rag covered almost all of her honey-colored hair.

"You're looking good, Harriet," I said, using her undercover name when she was at Urbana College of Magic. "You remember my boyfriend, Eddie?"

She nodded as she shook the vampire's hand heartily. "Good to see you again, Eddie,"

"Same here," Eddie replied.

"So," Robin asked as he put an arm around Brooke, "did you guys just get here?"

I nodded. "Are the people here just as creepy?" I asked my brother.

"Yep! I think the guy running the merry-go-round is a little baked. Hey, do you guys want to join us on the Ferris wheel?"

"Sure! What about you, babe?" Eddie asked me.

"I'd love to," I replied.

We all walked to the multi-colored, gigantic Ferris wheel. The young vampire manning the wheel had a coating of white powder around his nose. It wasn't cocaine, but the confectionary sugar from powdered doughnuts. "Shelly, has that guy been using?" my brother whispered to me.

"I'm not going to read his mind for you!" I hissed back at

him, even though I had done so already.

"Oh, please, Robin!" Brooke said in a disgusted voice. "You're off duty."

Robin shot my boyfriend a pleading look. "Come on, Eddie. A little help here."

Eddie pretended to wash his hands. "I am not getting involved!" he said.

The Ferris wheel operator demanded to see our wristbands. Apparently, he took the title, Ride Manager, on his name tag very seriously. When he knew that we were all legal, he pulled back a lever. The Ferris wheel turning slowly with a loud KA-CHUNK, KA-CHUCK! A bright green cart slid in between the hole in the wooden platform. The attendant unfastened the chain connected to the metal and wooden door.

Eddie and I sat down on one seat and pulled the metal bar down across our laps. Robin and Brooke sat across from us. The car began moving backward swiftly towards the top of the wheel. I peered over the edge of the cart and looked out over the fairgrounds. Eddie's carrot car looked like a spot of orange on the green lawn. A long, black tube snaked along the grass. "Ooh, the Tunnel of Love!" I turned to Eddie. "Let's go on that next!" I

had never been on a tunnel of love ride and was looking forward

to the cheesiness.

He shot a patronizing smile at me. The myth that

vampires can't cross water is totally bogus. In reality, my

boyfriend knew the water ride was going to be completely

campy. "I'd love to, Shelly," he said sarcastically.

I smiled as I shook my head at him. I continued to look at

the fairgrounds. Behind some of the dumpsters and

porta-potties, I noticed a large circle outlined in white. Strange, I

thought, I wonder if that's a new ride. Unfortunately, we were

coming towards the ground again so there was no way to tell

how big the circle was or anything about it.

Robin had been pointing out all of the fair's landmarks to

Brooke when he asked me if I had seen my stalker. "Do you

know anything about him, Shelly?"

"I do," Eddie said. He told Robin about the incident at the

mall and what he knew about Boko. "But you don't have to worry

about Shelly's safety. I gave her a Scorpion XL for protection."

Robin's face blanched. "You're not carrying, are you?" he

asked me.

"Not at the present moment!" I said. "I left it in Eddie's car along with my purse."

"You can't be carrying a concealed weapon without a permit!"

"Robin, I do have a permit!" Eddie protested.

"I know, but I'm pretty sure Shelly doesn't. Hand the gun over to me later on tonight," Robin ordered.

I glared at Eddie. *Why did you have to tell him about the gun?* I sent the telepathic message with a hint of irritation. Eddie shrugged. He knows how annoying my brother can be when he goes into his full-blown cop mode. *It just slipped out, babe. I'm sorry.*

At least, you didn't tell him about the stun gun. Who knows what laws I would have broken with that one? "Okay, Robin," I said giving up the fight. "I'll give the gun to you when we get off this ride."

"That is if we ever get off this ride!" Brooke said. Only she noticed our car had stopped at the very top of the wheel. She was looking down at the ride's operating booth. The young vampire was not at the controls. "Where did he go?"

"Maybe he went to the bathroom," Eddie suggested.

"Or maybe he went to go get something to eat or drink," Robin said. "Whatever the reason, he just left us here. At least, he could have told us or something!"

Eddie leaned over the car's railing as far as he could without falling out. He stared down at the controls, taking only a few seconds to locate the main lever. He wished there was some way to see if the lever was stuck. "Hey, Robin, do you think that you can generate a vine of some sort?"

"I can try," Robin said. Using his magical talent of chlorokinesis, my brother created a vine from a nearby munco tree. These trees have many magical properties such as consistently orange leaves and very strong vines.

"Better make it about fifty-feet long," Eddie told him. Robin nodded as he grabbed his end of the vine and began pulling it into the cart. All the while, the vine kept on getting longer. Finally, it came to the desired length, and Robin told it to break off from the tree.

Eddie took the vine from Robin and tied one end into a

slipknot. Then he threw the vine over the side. "Come on! Catch!" he told it as he waved it back and forth.

"What are you doing?" Robin asked him.

"I'm going to try to catch the vine on the main control lever. Hopefully, the lever is just stuck, and maybe I can pull it loose." Eddie gave a sharp tug on the vine as the loop slipped over the lever pull. Nothing happened. He gave a harder tug, but the lever didn't budge. He tried again, this time pulling with all of his vampire strength, but the only good that did was send the vine snapping back into his face. "Frig!" he said, letting go of the all-natural green rope. That was going to leave a mark on him. Eddie settled back into the seat, holding his hand up to his bruised cheek. It would only sting for awhile because vampires are fast healers.

A worried look spread over Brooke's face. "What's wrong with it? Why couldn't you loosen it?" she asked Eddie.

"I don't know. It felt like a strongman magic spell with some type of ward spell mixed in," he replied. Ward spells are designed to prevent other forms of magic from being performed.

I peered down towards the operating booth and noticed

for the first time that someone was lying face down on the grass behind the Ferris wheel. "Hey, guys!" I said. "I think I found our ride manager." I attempted to get a mind-reading from him. "This can't be good."

Everyone looked at me in alarm. "What do you mean?" Brooke asked me.

"Oh, just that he's not getting up anytime soon!"

So, there we were. Stuck on the tip-top of a Ferris wheel because someone put a spell on the controls, and the guy who was operated the ride was currently lying completely dead on the grass. I leaned against Eddie. "Any ideas about getting down?" I asked him.

"Jumping is completely out of the question 'cause I really don't want to break any bones," he said.

"Maybe someone will notice the Ferris wheel isn't moving and come to rescue us!" I said hopefully.

Brooke had closed her eyes as her brow furrowed in thought. "There's way too much magic on this ride!" she murmured quietly.

"What do you mean?" I asked.

"I'm channeling a very basic magic-seeking spell."

"Are you picking up anything?" Robin asked her.

She frowned. "I think I know why nobody is coming to help. Look on the ground!"

We all peered down. People passed under the Ferris wheel and even waved to us with a smile on their faces. No one with wings or the ability to fly came up to help. Eddie immediately realized what was going on. "Son of a hellhound!" he said as he snapped his fingers. "He's got the ride under an illusion spell."

"Think you can disarm it, Brooke?" my brother asked the elfin enchantress.

She shook her head. "I don't have that sort of power, Robin," she said.

I looked over at Eddie. He certainly didn't have the power either to disable the spell or whatever that was. "What's an illusion spell?" I asked them. Why am I always the last to know these things? "Can anyone on the ground hear or see us at all?"

Eddie shook his head. "This spell distorts the senses. To outsiders, they probably only see the Ferris wheel working properly."

Super. There's nothing like being stuck on the top of the Ferris wheel for hours and hours on end. I leaned against the vampire because there was nothing to do but wait.

Everyone was silent for a long time. We had apparently run out of topics to talk about other than the weather. Eddie put his arm around me, and then he and Robin shared a conspiratorial grin.

I suddenly felt the car start to swing back and forth. "Stop rocking the car, Eddie and Robin!" I snapped irritably at the guys.

Robin looked at the vampire. "She read your mind, didn't she?" When Eddie nodded, he shook his head. "Dang it! I hate when she does that!"

"Tell me about it!" Eddie said as he continued to rock the car. Suddenly, he felt a sharp elbow into his side. "Shelly, what was that for?" he asked.

"You know exactly why!" I replied.

"Okay, Okay!" Eddie said, holding up his hands in surrender. "I'll stop rocking the car. Just for you, babe." He leaned over and kissed me.

"Thank you, Eddie," I said. Then I leaned over to Brooke

and whispered to her, "Elbow to the side. That's how you keep them in line."

She laughed. "I'll keep that in mind, Shelly."

A few seconds later, I hardly noticed the gentle rocking of the cart. Probably it was just Eddie and Robin being stupid and trying to scare me and most likely Brooke. Soon, the rocking became more and more violent. "Edgar Van Helsing, stop rocking the freaking car!" I hissed at the vampire. "It's scaring the crap out of me!"

"I'm not rocking the cart, Shelly," he said honestly.

"Neither am I," Robin added.

Someone or something was causing the cart to rock on its own. We were at least thirty feet above the ground with no safe way to get down.

"I can do a teleportation spell," Brooke said as the car almost swung upside. "But I can only take one other person with me!"

Eddie nodded. He knew that teleportation spell can only transport two people at a time. "Go. Take Robin with you!" he told her.

Brooke nodded as she clung to my brother. She closed her eyes and whispered, "Travel!" They disappeared in a cloud of white smoke.

"Eddie!" I screamed as the cart tipped fully upside down. Our bodies lurched forward onto the metal bar. I would have slipped under it if not been for Eddie grabbing my arm. He pulled me up. I threw my arms around him as tightly as I could.

"Hang on!" he said as he gave the bar a hard shove forward, once the car turned upright again. The locks on the bar cracked as it opened. With his arms wrapped tightly around me, we jumped out of the cart.

"What are you doing?" I screamed involuntarily as we plunged down. I managed to open my eyes as the ground came up at us. Great, my brains were going to spill out when we hit the wooden-covered metal platform.

The vampire let go of me with one arm and shouted, "Citadel!" A pale green force field encircled Eddie and me just inches before we hit the platform. We bounced twice off the platform as if we were in a big beach ball.

I found myself on top of my boyfriend as we lay on the

grass a few feet away from the Ferris wheel. The force field disappeared within a few seconds, and I rolled off. Standing on my feet, I looked up at where we had been sitting. The Ferris wheel wasn't operating at all. I looked over at Eddie. "I thought you said that people from the ground were blinded by the spell's power," I told him. "Because it sure doesn't look like the Ferris Wheel is moving at all."

"The spell must have worn off, babe, when we got off," the vampire replied.

"More like 'jumped' off," I mumbled as I brushed myself off. The force field ball had cushioned our fall so neither of us received even a scratch. I glanced at where I had seen the body of the ride Nazi. Robin was talking on his cell phone while Brooke was clearing away bystanders. A long wooden stake had gone clean through his heart and protruded from the back of the young vampire. A pool of blood-soaked the grass around him. "I can't look at this, Eddie," I said in a hoarse whisper as bile started to creep up my throat.

Chapter Eight:

Eddie and I Fall Off the Love Boat

Eddie put his arm around me and started to take me away

from the scene of the crime. Several uniformed police officers

were arriving at the base of the Ferris wheel. One of the officers

asked if we had seen anything suspicious during our ride, and

we said no.

Finally, Eddie suggested that the two of us go for a ride on

the Tunnel of Love. He thought it would take my mind off the

crime scene. We walked to the ride where the attendant, an old

fairy woman, smiled at us. "Are you ready for the ride of

loooove?" she asked us, prolonging the last word in the sentence

in a desperate attempt to make the ride less campy.

Eddie and I nodded. Both of us had a feeling that she had

been at this job a little too long.

"There were a couple of kids who came on the ride a little

while ago, but I really don't think they appreciated the value of this ride," the lady prattled on as she unlocked the turnstile for us. We followed her to the beginning of the ride where rushing water pumped into a twenty-foot, plastic and metal tunnel that was covered in black Flexi-steel, a very strong steel that can be bent into any possible shape.

Eddie and I sat in the cheap, little boat, and the woman pushed us off. There was no bar to hold in. If the rapidly moving water tipped us over, we were screwed. The boat began its course down a path flickering with multi-colored strobe lights. I drew close to my boyfriend as a tape of incredibility effective scary haunted house noises and creepy organ music played over various amplifiers. Talk about misleading advertisements!

"Are you scared?" Eddie whispered as he put an arm around me.

"No!" I lied. I could sense his smile as I leaned my head against his shoulder. Had I been here all alone, then yes, I would've been terrified. Something wasn't right about this ride. I heard a splash in the water behind us and involuntarily turned around in my seat. The strobe lights were of no help, and I wasn't sure if my imagination was playing tricks on me or if someone had followed us here.

Is there something wrong, Shelly? Eddie asked me subliminally. The music and creepy haunted house noises were playing too loud for us to have a decent conversation.

I thought I heard something in the water behind us! I heard the splashing again and then a loud moaning sound that did not come from any loudspeaker. Like in a bad horror movie, the lights and the recordings abruptly stopped. It was then I began picking up someone's brain waves from behind us, and they were not good at all.

It's never a comforting thought to learn someone wants you for lunch. The thoughts I was receiving increased as we sat in the boat. Eddie, someone wants to eat us! I sent the telepathic message with trepidation.

Using his ability to sense the thermal heat outlines of creatures, the vampire looked around for anybody else in the tunnel. Suddenly, he picked out two pale blue shapes making their way towards us. "Holy smokes!" he said under his breath.

He looked at me. *Don't move!*

My body froze, but my mind didn't. I tried to figure out what we were dealing with. They were undead, that was for sure. I knew they weren't vampires because vampires don't get their blood from biting the necks of the living. It's way too messy and illegal. Eddie saw pale blue outlines which meant no werewolves were in here.

I would have screamed if Eddie hadn't clamped a hand over my mouth when I caught a glimpse of one of the creatures' faces. The clown's makeup was hanging off his half-burnt face, and his faded clown suit had huge burn marks all over it. But it was his eyes that scared me the most. The irises were completely glazed over like he was dead. The realization hit me like a brick wall when I remembered what a blue heat rating was. Dead. To be more specific, the living dead. "Zombies!" I whispered, my voice shaking.

I heard two low splashes as I read the minds of the zombies. They had gone underwater, but I had no idea where. That's the problem with telepathy. When someone leaves a room, a telepath can't read their thoughts. Pretty much, any type of physical barrier stops it. "Eddie, they're somewhere under the water."

"Keep still, Shelly!" Eddie told me in a low voice. "Zombies are attracted to movement, especially connected to noise." He kept looking around for them to reappear. "We need to get out of here!" The urgency in his voice was unmistakable.

"No kidding!" Knowing the nature of zombies, I asked Eddie if zombies eat vampires.

"Living, dead, undead! Zombies really don't really care where their next meal comes from."

Suddenly, the boat tipped forward, and Eddie and I found ourselves toppling head over heels into the water. The next thing I knew, I was gasping for air as I stood in the murky liquid.

Eddie had come up next to me and was holding the boat up with one hand. *Shelly, the zombies are on the other side of the boat. We are going to swim under the boat and climb up on the land. We've got to be quiet. You ready?*

I managed a nod. I grabbed his hand as I plugged my nose and held my breath. I submerged again and swam along beside the vampire. I had no idea he was such a strong swimmer. He would make the perfect lifeguard.

Once we were on the other side of the boat, Eddie climbed up on the ledge without making a sound. Then he grabbed me by the wrists and pulled me to safety. Unfortunately, I wasn't as quiet as my boyfriend.

The zombies stopped searching for their meals when they heard the splash. Making a loud, deep-throated moan, they heaved the boat at us with superhuman strength.

There are times when I'm so glad that Eddie used to be a wizard, and this was one. He stepped in front of me to block the impact of the hit. "Duracell!" he shouted as two blue balls of energy shot out from the palms of his hands. The energy sent the boat back into our assailants. The sickening sound of broken bones and brains splattering echoed throughout the building. The vampire grabbed my hand as we ran to the exit at the other end of the tunnel. We both leapt onto the ground.

Screams of "Zombie clowns!" were erupting throughout the fairgrounds. We looked around at the stumbling dead clowns chasing families. Game booths were tipped over, and food from popcorn and cotton machines covered the grounds.

A zombie satyr had cornered a mother and her little girl next to the merry-go-round. The painted smile on his face was grinning evil. "Stay here!" Eddie ordered me. He lifted the large metal cover of a cotton candy machine and ran to help the family. "Lady, cover your kid's eyes!" he ordered the frightened mother. "Hey, you!" he shouted to the zombie. Once it turned to face him, he threw the cover like a Frisbee. The force of the Eddie's vampire strength severed the top of the zombie's head. Once he knew the mother and daughter were safe, Eddie ran back to me. "Let's get out of here!"

Somehow I made it back to the car. I was shivering in my wet clothes, but my mind was numb with horror from the carnage. Once we had sped out of the parking lot, I glanced back in the side mirror to see the blue and red emergency lights at the fair. The murder of the Ferris wheel operator was going to have to be put on hold. I tried not to think of the zombie brains all over the grass.

"The police will be able to stabilize them, Shelly," Eddie told me as he read the sickened look on my face. We were turning onto my street. "They've got tranquilizers to knock out the zombies, and antidote for those who might have been bitten." He knew I was really upset at what had happened. "Shelly," he said softly as he gently squeezed my hand, "that mom and her kid were in trouble. I had to destroy the zombie's brain. It was the only way I could stop it."

I nodded vaguely as my stomach churned at the image of the decapitation replaying in my mind. I doubled over in my seat. "I think I'm going to throw up!" And I did. As soon as I was done, I looked up with tears in my eyes. "I'm so sorry, Eddie," I mumbled as I tried not to look at the pile I had created on the car floor. Thankfully, we had just pulled into my driveway.

Eddie put the car in park and then put his arm around me. "It's all right, babe," he said. "Don't worry about it. I'll clean it up when I get home." We got out of the car, and he walked me to my door. He kissed me on the forehead. "Get some rest, Shelly. You look like you need it. I'll talk to you later."

"Thanks, Eddie," I mumbled. I wanted to kiss him on the lips, but I decided against it with the taste of vomit still lingering in my mouth. I fished around for the keys in my purse and then proceeded to unlock the door. "Good night, Eddie," I told the vampire as we waved goodbye.

"'Night, Shell!" he said. Once he made sure I was safely inside, he headed back to his car.

Chapter Nine:
And the Dumpster Diving Award Goes To…

Sitting on the edge of my kitchen table was a pixie in her late teens. "Whoa, Shelly!" Raine Cloude noticed my disheveled state. "What happened to you?"

"Eddie and I fell off the love boat!" I said to the pixie as I walked into my bedroom. After shuffling around my dresser drawers, I found a blue sweatshirt, a pair of jeans and clean undergarments.

"I thought you and Eddie were going to the carnival," Raine asked as she buzzed over my bed, her transparent dragonfly wings whipping up a cloud of golden dust.

The pixie and her busy family of twenty siblings and her single mom lived in the flower garden next to my house. My 78-year-old landlord, Simon Boer, had planted five flower beds around my little two-three bedroom housing community last spring. But rheumatoid arthritis in the elderly satyr's hands and knees had interrupted his plans of maintaining them. He asked the Cloude family to live on his rental properties and take care of the flowerbeds.

"We did."

"Then how did you get all wet?"

I wiped away a piece of wet hair that had fallen in my eyes. "Let me shower and get out of these wet clothes, and I'll tell you what happened!" I said as I headed towards the bathroom.

"Okey-dokey!" Raine flew over to the couch and flicked on the television to watch a rerun of her favorite show.

I added an extra ten- minutes to my usual fifteen-minute shower. Who knew what creepy things lurked in the waters of the tunnel of love? Once my body was clean enough to pass any kind of health inspection, I changed into dry clothes and brushed my teeth. Then I scooped up the wet clothes and did a quick load of laundry to get rid of the rest of the grossness.

Raine shut off the television and turned to face me as I

plopped into my gray recliner. "So, tell me everything!" she said.

I told her what had happened at the carnival, leaving out the gross details of the zombie slaughter. I didn't want a reenactment of the scene in Eddie's car. Then my thoughts turned to my winged horse. I was probably going to have a huge vet's bill for Jordan's broken wing. "Did Dr. Montgomery call me at all?"

Raine shook her head. "Sorry, Shelly." She knew how anxious I was about my horse's condition. Then her brow furrowed in thought as she tried to remember something. She snapped her fingers. "That's it! I saw something strange at the fair tonight before the zombie attacks."

"Other than the usual freaks?"

Her laugh rang through the room like a melodious song. "No, I was near the edge of the fairgrounds with Eva." Eva was one of the pixie's more responsible siblings. "We saw this kid, a vampire, chanting inside a circle outlined with dog bones. He was holding a really old book in his hands."

This struck me as odd. Was this kid responsible for raising the zombies? I wondered. "So, what happened next?"

"His cell phone rang, and I guess he was getting a bad signal or something because he walked away. Then Eva and I left the fairgrounds."

I took off the hair elastic I had slipped over my wrist and pulled my hair back into a wet ponytail. If that kid was raising dead clowns, I needed to know all about this zombie business. The library is open twenty-four hours, and I had plenty of time to do some research on the living dead. "Hey, Raine, do you want to come with me to the library?" I offered.

"I'd love to," Raine replied as she got off the couch and hitched a ride on my purse. "There's nothing on TV anyway!"

I parked Eddie's car in the lot across the street. We walked through the front doors. Fortunately, the public computer room was practically empty, with the exception of the creepy guy getting his daily porn fix. We sat as far away from him as possible. I logged on the computer with my library barcode number. Using the word "zombie" on an Internet search engine, we found some very useful information about zombie raising.

Back in the 1700s, a Welkie by the name of Archibald

Hawthorne dabbled in this illegal art of raising the dead while teaching at a small school for underage wizards and enchantresses. According to Hawthorne's infamous book, On Necromancy (where had I seen that before?) once a person completes the ritual of the zombie curse, the zombies arise from the place where they died, not from their graves, and go on the rampage. It doesn't matter how long they've been dead because their bodies will almost regenerate. Unfortunately, Hawthorne's zombie raising got him into big-time trouble when he lost control of the zombies. At the time, the creatures viciously attacked the king of Urbana and his family.

I cringed as I read how the head wizard of the Court had Hawthorne drawn and quartered for his recklessness. What a nasty way to go. After this ancient debacle, the practice and teaching of necromancy were forever banned from this realm.

"I remember my granddad telling me about this guy when he worked at a school for Welkies," Raine said in a low voice. "Apparently all Welkies are taught about the hazards of zombie raising in the freshman Dark Magic classes. You can lose your magic privileges if you raise zombies."

"Why?" I asked, mainly out of curiosity.

"Because zombies can only be under the necromancer's control for so long. Once he loses control, all hell breaks loose," the pixie said.

"Oh!" I was growing tired of reading. Then I remembered what Eddie told me about Boko: he had his magic privileges suspended before his arrest. I went back to the search engine main's page and typed in my stalker's name. A list of articles appeared on the page.

Raine and I glanced down at some of the headlines when something caught her eye. "Shelly!" she almost squealed as she pointed to the headline reading: Welkie Suspected in Zephyr Carnival Deaths. "Looks like an article about the Zephyr Summer Moon Festival."

I opened up the link. About fifty years ago, a large traveling clown troupe was trapped in a burning building on the fairgrounds. Their manager, Ahab Boko, was the only survivor. I frowned in thought. This Boko guy had a connection to the fairgrounds. Did he do the zombie raising? He was certainly capable of it, but I needed something more conclusive. "Let's go look at the microfiche for this date," I told the pixie. I hit the print button on the article. After I paid for my copies, Raine and I went to the microfiche room.

Just as we got ourselves situated, the song, "You Sexy Thing," echoed throughout the room. I dug my cell phone out of my purse and flipped it open. "Yes, Eddie?" I said into the receiver with a huge smile.

"How are you feeling, babe?" Eddie asked.

"Better. In fact, I'm at the library with Raine."

"Why?"

"Doing a little research on zombies and stalkers."

"Really? Sounds interesting." He paused slightly. "Why don't I meet you there, and then maybe you and I can go for some ice cream?"

"Ooh! Sounds delish! See you later."

"Love ya!"

"Love you, too!" I hung up the phone as Raine found the correct box of microfilm. Once I inserted the film into the machine, I began scrolling down until I saw the front-page article about the fire. There was nothing new in the article. Skipping past the next few weeks of news about the famous Wixom War, new inventions appearing on the scene of the worlds, and other things, I finally noticed an editorial about the fire. The picture showed a black-and-white photograph of a beautiful nymph, Claudia Woodstock, the article's author. She was fueling a rumor that went around concerning the fire. The clowns went on strike until Boko raised their wages. Boko apparently refused to give in to their demands, lured his employees into the building, and then set it ablaze. "Whoa!" I said. "This guy's nuts!"

"Interesting," said a voice into my ear.

Raine and I both jumped up. "Edgar Van Helsing!" I whirled around in my seat the second I felt the vampire's hand resting on my shoulder. "Don't scare us like that!"

Eddie smiled at me. "Sorry about that, Shelly." He grabbed an empty wooden chair from a nearby table. He turned it around and sat down, resting his arms on the back of the chair. "So, what did you find?" He listened without interrupting as Raine and I took turns telling him what the pixie saw at the fair and what we learned here at the library. "I wonder if Boko bumped that reporter off. I vaguely remember reading about her apparent suicide a few weeks after the fire."

I scrolled down past another week of boring news until I spotted the news article the vampire was talking about. "Reporter Commits Suicide:" the short paragraph read, "Claudia Woodstock, the reporter who covered the Zephyr Circus fire, was found dead in her bathtub. Police have ruled her death a suicide. I stopped reading the article and glanced over at Eddie. "You really think it's possible he killed her?" I asked him.

He nodded. "When I was tracking him down, I read her autopsy report. It looked like someone had changed the cause of death."

I looked up in disbelief. "You serious, Eddie?" I asked him. "Did you tell anyone?"

He shrugged. "Nah, I was new at the bounty hunter gig. I didn't want to intrude upon a closed police case. Plus, I had no medical background to support my suspicions."

"That's it!" I said snapping my fingers together. The ghost and the vampire looked at me strangely. "Boko's the one who raised the zombies."

"Boko does have a strong connection to the fairgrounds,"

Eddie said. "But that doesn't mean he was the one who raised

the zombies!"

"What do you mean?" I asked, surprised. I thought that

raising the dead could only be done if you're a Welkie."

Eddie shook his head. "Anyone with the proper tools and

the right chant can raise the dead. The key thing is keeping them

under control!"

I shut off the microfiche and put the box back on the shelf.

"I'm ready for that ice cream you promised me," I told him.

"Oh, Shelly, I took your advice and spoke to Luken."

"I hope you booted him out," Raine said. "He sounds like a

pig."

"He's has been officially kicked to the curb."

"Good!" Raine and I said at the same time.

"I'm just chock-full of good advice, Eddie," I said

He grinned at me as we all left the library. As we were

walking down the marble stairs leading down to the street, Raine

noticed a couple of kids smoking on the sidewalk. "That's the

kids I saw at the fair!" she whispered to Eddie and me. "I've got

to go!" The pixie flitted away leaving us alone with the kids.

"I know one of those kids," Eddie said. It was one of the campers he had been responsible for last year at Camp Coffin. Apparently, this kid was always getting into trouble, but his rich, lawyer dad always bailed him out. "Doug Bloodman!" he called down to the kids.

The blond-haired vampire kid whirled around to face Eddie. He looked like a wannabe rapper with his gold chain necklace and a backwards baseball cap. "Yo! Yo! What's up, Mr. E?"

"Nothing much," Eddie replied as a knowing smile crossed his face. "I heard that you and your friend were at the fair earlier tonight!"

The too-cool look vanished from Doug's face. "We didn't do anything wrong! It was a joke!" he said throwing up his hands in protest.

"Yeah, man!" the other kid in the hooded sweatshirt said in an almost hysterical voice. "The zombies were just supposed to scare people, not attack anybody!"

"I didn't say anything about zombies," Eddie said calmly.

Doug shot his friend a dirty look. He should associate

himself with brighter crayons in the box. "Naboth, you moron! That's how Mr. E. reels you into confessing!"

"Now that we know who raised the zombies," Eddie said, "mind telling us, what possessed you to do a stupid thing like that?"

"Uh," Doug replied hesitantly, "Rocky dared us to do it. It's the only way for Naboth and me to join the Hammerheads."

I rolled my eyes at the kids. The Hammerheads are a group of fifteen-to-seventeen-year-olds wanna-be gang bangers. Their biggest run-in with the law was that they were warned not to spray graffiti on government property. "You raised zombies just so you could be in a gang!" I nearly shouted. "Did your brains go on vacation?"

Doug began slowly backing away. "Man, Mr. E., your girlfriend's a psycho."

"You would be a little crazy too if zombies threw at a boat at you," Eddie said to Doug.

"Nobody was supposed to get hurt," Naboth protested. "It was just a joke!"

"Exactly how many zombies did you two raise?" Eddie

demanded.

"Umm—A couple?" Doug guessed. He had no idea what he had gotten himself into.

"Try twelve!" the older vampire said.

"Okay, so we raised a few zombies. What's the big deal?" Naboth asked.

"The big deal is raising zombies is illegal," I said to the ignoramuses, empowering my newfound knowledge. "One can only control the zombies for so long. After that, all hell breaks loose."

"What spell did you two use?" Eddie asked.

"Some spell from a book called *On Necromancy,*" Doug answered. What he forgot to mention was where he got the censored book. Unfortunately for vampire kids, they really can't control blocking telepathy.

After I found out where Doug and Naboth got the book, I was livid. "You're the little twerps who stole the library books the other day!" I nearly lunged at Doug and Naboth in a failed attempt to wring their scrawny necks. "Was that part of your gang initiation, too?"

"Shelly, don't kill them," Eddie gently advised me. The last thing that he wanted was to bail me out of jail when I get arrested for justifiable homicide. "She works at the library," he explained to Doug and Naboth.

"We'll bring the books back!" Naboth said, "but not all of them!"

"And why not?" I asked through gritted teeth.

"An old wizard saw us performing the spell and asked to see the book," Naboth said. "Doug gave it to him, and he threw it into the dumpster right next to the magic circle, after he tore out a couple pages." Too bad for us, the kids gave very sketchy descriptions of the guy.

Eddie and I exchanged glances. If the guy was Boko, then who knows what spell he was planning on using. The only way we would ever find out was to hunt down that book.

About fifteen minutes later after we took the kids downtown to the police station where they were turned over to their parents Eddie and I were standing in front of a huge red dumpster at the edge of the eerily empty fairgrounds. The white

105

circle of chicken and dog bones I had seen from atop the Ferris wheel was scattered all around the dumpster. I remembered reading about magic circles when I was a college librarian. Just as long as a person stays inside a magic circle, he is safe from any side effects of a spell.

Eddie was staring at the dumpster. He wrinkled his nose at the overpowering smell of stale hot dogs, burnt popcorn, and other unpleasant odors that accompany the carnival. "There is no way I'm searching through that dumpster to retrieve this book."

I looked at him, surprised at his unwillingness to look for a potentially dangerous book. "You will decapitate a zombie, but you refuse to go dumpster diving!"

"Hey, I have my priorities. Plus, I just bought these sneakers."

"Well, I'm not going in there," I protested. "It smells! You know how sensitive my stomach is."

Eddie rolled his eyes. "This coming from the woman who blew up a spider demon with a vaporizer?"

"And who knows what diseases lurk in there?" Then I

smiled as I got an idea. I would coax him with the anticipation of something special. "I'll get you a box of gourmet chocolates if you do it."

That piqued Eddie's interest. Anything sweet is his Scooby Snacks. "But don't put any of those disgusting apricot chocolates in the box."

"Deal!" I said as we shook hands.

Before pulling on a pair of disposable gloves we wisely brought with us, Eddie tossed back the plastic lid of the dumpster after retrieving flashlight from his magic black bag. "Hold the flashlight for me, babe." Then he leaped into the dumpster with a loud THUD! "Oh! This is disgusting!" he announced.

"Better you than me."

He chose to ignore my snide remark. "I think I stepped into a puddle of coffee and cola along with a batch of popcorn. We should have rented hazmat suits. Light, please!"

I peered into the dumpster as I turned on the bright flashlight. The powerful stench of garbage nearly knocked me off my feet. "Whoa! It stinks in here!"

"Believe me, it's no bed of roses down here," He looked at

the garbage around his feet. "God, don't people believe in using garbage bags anymore?" With the aid of the flashlight, he gingerly pawed through the piles of newspapers drenched in slush-puppy goo, rotten banana peels, half-eaten apples, overcooked corn dogs and doughboys, and other unsavory things one might find in a typical carnival dumpster.

"Found it!" he shouted as he held up an old leather-bound book covered with blue and pink pieces of cotton candy and something that looked suspiciously like a regurgitated combination of a chili dog and a fruit smoothie. He leaped out of the dumpster and closed the lid. "Those chocolates had better be good." He looked down at his feet. "Okay, these shoes will never be worn again."

I gingerly took the book away from him with gloved hands, holding it out as far as my arm could extend. There was no way the library would ever take back this book. I finally flipped through the pages to see what had been ripped out. I gave a short gasp when I saw the missing section. "I told you that Boko was raising zombies!"

Chapter Ten:

Amelia Gets a Psycho at Her Bridal Shower

It was a good thing I had the day off. All the excitement last night left me totally exhausted. At nine o'clock in the morning, Lisa's moving around woke me up. Amelia's bridal shower was at one o'clock this afternoon, and Lisa was hurrying to get things wrapped up. I threw my pillow over my head to block out the noises my best friend was making.

I finally dragged my butt out of bed at eleven. I was in the shower when I heard someone pounding on my front door. "Crap! Lisa probably locked herself out again." I shut off the water and threw on my teal bathrobe.

I opened the door. The only thing on my doorstep was a box. Nobody was around when I bent down to pick up the crudely wrapped box tied with string, but I got the feeling that someone was watching me from afar. The cardboard box felt damp, but the ground around it was dry.

I locked the door again and set the box on the kitchen table. There were no markings on the box to indicate who the present was for, and there was a rather pungent smell coming from it. It would have to wait until my shower was over.

When I went out to look at the box a few minutes later, I noticed a reddish puddle on the tablecloth where the box was sitting. "What the heck?" I asked myself. Taking a knife, I cut off the strings and opened the box.

When I was in high school, I almost threw up in biology when Mr. Jessup had us dissect a frog. Seeing any animal's innards still makes me queasy, but my stomach has matured a little bit since high school. I found myself staring into the vacant eyes of a disembodied chicken head. "Ohmigod!" I screamed. The box tumbled out of my hand and the head rolled across the kitchen floor leaving behind a trail of blood. I ran back into the bathroom and knelt before the porcelain throne. After my breakfast was flushed away, I forced myself to keep from gagging as I cleaned up the vileness.

Once that lovely chore was done, I decided to wrap

Amelia's gift in some wrapping paper with soft white doves flying around pink roses I had bought the day Dad and Amelia announced their engagement to keep my mind off the disgusting mail I received. After a few moments of scrambling for tape and scissors, I carefully wrapped up the jewelry box. I tapped a card and a silver bow and to the top of the present. "Shelly, you're a genius," I told myself as I admired my handiwork. "A creative genius!"

I checked my watch. I still had an hour to go before the bridal shower, but with the little surprise I had received, I was getting a little too anxious. There's nothing more unnerving than being home alone when you get an anonymous chicken head in the mail. I gathered up the present and my purse with both mine and Eddie's car keys and left the house.

Amelia's house is right next to my father's so I decided to park Eddie's car in Dad's driveway. That way all bridal shower guests would have plenty of room to park their animals. Lisa was helping a tall elf with short blond hair put a bright pink tablecloth on the dining room table when I went into Amelia's dining area.

"Hey, Shelly," Lisa said to me tersely. "I'm glad you're here early. Could you help Amelia prepare the vegetables for the veggie tray? Libby and I got everything else done."

"Uh, sure," I mumbled as I set my present on a side table next to the large beautiful wrapped present that no doubt came from Lisa. I wandered into the kitchen where I spotted Amelia washing a few pots in the kitchen sink. "Amelia, Lisa said you needed help with the vegetable tray," I said, announcing my presence.

Amelia turned around and greeted me with a huge smile. "Shelly," she said as she gave me a much-needed hug, "you're here early!"

"I thought you guys might need some help setting up the party." I lied. There was no need to tell her about my present. I nearly puked at the thought. I grabbed a paring knife from a kitchen drawer and began to slice cucumbers on the built-in cutting board that was attached to the kitchen island.

Amelia looked at me strangely. "Shelly," she asked, "are you feeling alright? You look a little pale." She used to be a registered nurse, and she can tell if someone is sick or not.

"Oh, no! I'm fine," I lied again. "I felt a little sick this morning."

"Do you need some medicine?"

I shook my head. As long as I could filter out the nasty image of the chicken head, I knew I was going to be alright. As I sliced a carrot into semi-round circles, I debated about leaving Eddie a message concerning the unpleasant present. Nah, I decided, it would just wake him up and worry him.

I didn't realize how quickly time flies when you're putting cream cheese on celery sticks. It's the most disgusting job when putting together a veggie tray. After I dumped the vegetable peels I into the garbage disposal, I took the tray out to the dining room where Amelia and twenty of her friends gathered around in small groups chatting and giggling. The only people I knew at the bridal shower were, of course, Amelia, Libby Elfstone, and Lisa. My friend, Creighton Horsefeathers, and her mother had to cancel at the last minute because Jamison Horsefeathers, the famous centaur comedian and Creighton's grandfather had fallen seriously ill earlier in the week. I couldn't chat with Lisa because she was busy hosting the bridal shower, and I really didn't know

Libby, even though she had been dating Bruce for a month.

Everything was going smoothly until all of the ladies

stopped talking when we heard someone pounding furiously at

the front door. "I know you're in there!" a drunken voice called

from outside. "You ruined my plan, you despicable librarian!"

On that note, everyone turned to look at me in horror.

Even though I couldn't read any of their minds, I could tell what

they were thinking just by the look on their faces: Shelly has

brought a patron who is well over three sheets to the wind. "That

would be for me! I'll be right back," I said as I moved quickly

away from my position at the dessert table.

I sprinted back to the kitchen and dug around in my purse

for a suitable weapon. Yes, I know what I was about to do was

stupid. Confronting a dangerous man is not exactly the smartest

thing to do. But what choice did I have? This fool was not going

to ruin my future stepmother's bridal shower. I found what I was

looking for: the stun gun Eddie had given me the night before.

There was a little rust at the top because it probably hadn't been

used since Eddie worked at the Agency. "God, I hope this

works!" I said as I turned it on.

I crouched by a window near the door and peered out. It wasn't your everyday bum. To be more specific, it was a drunk sorcerer who had been stalking me at work. Think Shelly, I told myself. How am I going to get rid of this guy without getting any of the ladies hurt? I dialed the police and told them about my situation.

As soon as I was assured by the dispatcher an officer would be right over, Boko began smashing the flower pots that were outside the porch as he began ranting about how I had ruined his plan. It truly is amazing to hear how easily your name can be paired up with various swear words.

"Shelly," Lisa hissed as she came into the kitchen, "what in the world is going on? Everyone is scared to death because some nutcase is ranting on Amelia's porch. Who is this guy, and why did you invite him to the bridal shower?"

"Do you think I would invite someone like that to any occasion?" I said as I glanced out the door. "To answer your question, he's been stalking me for about a week now." After seeing the horrified look on Lisa's face, I gave her the Reader's

Digest Condensed version of what had been going on. "I've called the police, and now I just need an idea on how to get him under control." Then an idea hit me. Lisa had the power of photokinesis. "Think you can blast him with a light ray, Lis?"

"You mean blind him?"

I nodded. "I'll use Eddie's trusty stun gun to make sure he doesn't get away!"

Lisa looked a bit unsure. "Okay," she said as she reached for the doorknob, "One. Two. Three!" She swung the door open with one hand. A ray of bright light shot out of the other palm like a rocket.

Boko screamed in agony as he covered his eyes. He staggered backward, groping around for something sturdy to prevent him from falling off the fenceless porch. The next two things happened simultaneously.

First, I let him have it with my stun gun. Electricity flowed out of the weapon quickly but rebounded back to me when Boko used a force field spell to prevent himself from possible electrocution. I gave a small shriek as two electric shocks ran through my body. The tops of my knuckles were burning, and I instinctively let go of the gun. Later, I came to the conclusion that

I must have turned my hand towards the sorcerer the moment he

put a force field around himself. Clutching my injured hand, I

never saw Boko vanish from sight. "Where did he go?" I asked

Lisa.

She shrugged. "I never saw him leave. And neither did the

ladies. He just disappeared!" She was pointing to the gathering

of women peering out from the kitchen. "We're fine," Lisa called

to them as a cheery, fake smile appeared across her face. She

then turned to me. "How's your hand?"

"It's fine," I replied, shrugging off the throbbing pain. "You

go back inside and tend to the party. I'll stay out here and wait for

the police."

A few minutes later, my brother's green and black dragon

landed on the side of the street. Robin shook his head the

moment he saw me sitting on the porch. Sliding off Cornelius, he

walked up the driveway. "I take it the ladies didn't care for the

male stripper."

I groaned at his remark. Did every guy think that all bridal showers involve something sexual? "No, it was that Boko guy?"

Robin pushed his sunglasses on top of his head as he took out a small notebook and a pen from his inside coat pocket. He glanced around and noticed the stun gun on the porch. "Is that Boko's?" he asked.

I shook my head. "Eddie gave it to me for my protection," I told him what had happened, but left out the part concerning the chicken head.

Robin picked it up and inspected it carefully. "Shelly, you do realize this stun gun is almost twenty-years-old?"

"You're kidding!"

"Sorry, Shelly, but this stun gun hasn't been in commission for twenty years. I'm going to have to ticket Eddie for having a non-updated stun gun."

About two hours later, I was heading back to Amelia's. After confiscating the stun gun and asking me more questions, Robin told me to go down to the police station to file a restraining order on Boko. My brother insisted I leave everything to the police. Since I was the one possessing the stun gun, my credit card now had a $113.00 charge for a stun gun violation.

I parked the car across the street and peered out the window at Amelia's house. Apparently, everyone had left the party. The only animal in the yard was the giant white eagle who belonged to Amelia. I gave a great sigh. I had ruined the bridal shower and wasn't even there to see it. My heart ached. Might as well face the music. I got out of the car and jogged across the street. The only good thing about this whole situation was Boko was nowhere in sight.

Amelia greeted me at the door. She gasped when she saw the burn mark on my hand. "What happened to your hand, Shelly?" she asked me. Grabbing my wrist, the former nurse led me to the kitchen island and had me sit on a stool. "Shelly, is that an electrical burn?" she asked as she inspected my wound.

I nodded as she left the kitchen. Moments later, she was sitting next to me, rubbing some magical aloe lotion on my hand. The lotion started healing right away as the red sparks of magic danced all over the burn.

"There's some leftover punch in the fridge, sweetie. Would you like some?" Amelia offered. Once I nodded, she used her telekinesis to get a glass from the cupboard and brought it over to the counter. Then she forced the refrigerator door to open by itself and brought the glass pitcher filled to the top with leftover red punch. She did all of this without moving from her seat.

I took a sip of the lovely homemade punch and felt much better. "I'm really sorry about ruining your bridal shower, Amelia," I told her.

"Don't worry about it, Shelly. Nobody got seriously hurt, and the man left. Who is he?" Amelia got up and cut a piece of cake. "I saved a piece of cake for you."

I smiled as I took a bite out of the vanilla cake covered in purple and white creamy frosting. This was one of those times I was so glad she was going to be my stepmother. Even though I had to leave the party unexpectedly, Amelia had saved me some punch and cake. I knew that I had to tell her what was going on lately, and I did. I sipped my third glass of punch as I wrapped up my saga. "So, now this guy's stalking me because I had him arrested. I think he hurt Jordan, Robin's confiscated the gun and the taser which Eddie gave me for my protection, and now we—Eddie and I—think this guy Boko has access to a necromancy spell."

Amelia took a sip of the tea she had made while I told my story. "Do you think this man might use that spell against you?"

"I don't know. He might use it against anyone. He is a loose cannon." I cupped my head in my hands. "I should never have reported the guy in the first place."

Amelia gave me a hug. "Shelly, you did the right thing the first time. You've got a good head on your shoulders, and you'll find a way to stop him." Even though she has never had children, Amelia sure knows how to give motherly advice.

I nodded. I had to think of something to get rid of this stalker, but my brain couldn't come up with any bright ideas at the moment. "Did you like the gift I gave you, Amelia?" I asked, changing the subject.

"I don't know," she replied with a smile. "I haven't opened it yet. I was waiting for you." She got up and retrieved my present from the dining room. Her face was aglow as she took off the wrapping paper and pulled the jewelry box from the cardboard container. "It's lovely, Shelly! Did your father tell you to get this for me?"

"No.Why?"

"Well, last month, we were in the mall, and I tried to convince him to buy me this exact jewelry box. Shelly, this is the best bridal shower gift I've ever received. I'll definitely be putting all my jewelry in here."

Finally, the one thing I had been worrying about all this week was laid to rest. Amelia really loved the gift I gave her; not because I was trying to oust Lisa's expensive gift, but because it came from my heart. I really didn't want to go back to my house. Instead, I wanted to spend time with Amelia.

When I got home that afternoon, I took a much-needed nap. There was no chicken head to greet me when I stepped through my door, only a message on my answering machine. It was from Dr. Montgomery. Tears blinded my eyes as the veterinarian told me the prognosis wasn't good for Jordan. There was very little chance she would ever be able to fly again without very expensive surgery. Unless I wanted to go into major debt, I could never afford it.

As I lay on the couch, I thought about all the good times I

had with Jordan. She was a good winged horse, and patient, too.

When I first got her, I had never ridden a horse before, much less

one with wings. My butt had never been as sore as it was the

first dozen times she bucked me off. We flew everywhere

together, but now there was a possibility that our flying days

were over. My home felt like a Heartbreak Hotel. After tossing

and turning on the couch and staining the pillow with my tears, I

finally fell asleep.

Chapter Eleven:

Zombies Calling!

The wailing moans woke me up with a start. It was after seven, and the Zephyrian sun had already sunk low on the darkened horizon. The rising moon cast eerie shadows outside the sliding glass door. I lay motionless, trying to keep my heart from pounding, as four zombie clowns stomped outside my house. One was a satyr, his decomposing horns dripping with some kind of goo. The other three were a horribly burnt elf, a centaur with only half a face, and a fairy with one of his arms hanging by a bloody thread.

I hadn't bothered to turn on any lights in my house, and so I had the cover of darkness. What do I now? I asked myself. What do I know about zombies? They are raised from the dead by a necromancer, are super strong, but not very bright without all of their gray matter in place. I slid off the couch and crab-walked to the kitchen, keeping a low profile.

I reached up and grabbed my cell phone and dialed my boyfriend's number. "Come on! Come on, Eddie! Please, pick up the freaking phone!" I mumbled as the vampire's voicemail babbled on and on. I left a frantic message and hung up. After five minutes of waiting for Eddie's number to appear on the caller ID, I called him a second and third time but still was sent directly to his voicemail each time. Why wasn't he picking up?

I grabbed my purse off the kitchen table and prepared to venture outside when I realized I needed something to arm myself. Zombies moaned outside my house. After a frantic look around, I decided on a fire extinguisher. Even with all the fire safety, I had learned in school, the only thing I knew about fire extinguishers was they were red and put out fires. But this baby might be able to pack a pretty good punch.

I swung open the door, and two of the zombies greeted me with more guttural wails and moans. I almost went into cardiac arrest when I read the creatures' minds. The necromancer, or "Master" as they called him, had instructed them to kill me. Yea, the zombies even mentioned my full name in their thoughts. Not a good sign.

Flinging my purse over my shoulder, I swung my make-shift weapon at the zombie centaur and chopped off its front legs. It made a painful cry as it crumbled right in front of me. The dead elf swatted clumsily at me, but then I remembered what Eddie had told me about zombies. You have to destroy the brain in order to kill them. I walloped the next zombie with the fire extinguisher right upside the head. The head flew off into the bushes, and the zombie stood stock-still for a few moments.

This opportunity gave me the chance to sprint towards the car. Slamming the driver's door shut, I fumbled for the car keys inside my purse. "Found them," I said as I jammed the key into the ignition.

The only thing that happened was the THUD on the roof of the car. A zombie's head appeared in front of the windshield, and I let out a horrified scream. "Come on, come on, you frigging piece of junk!" I said to the car as I desperately tried to turn on the engine. This was not the time and place for it to stall on me. I hit Eddie's number on speed dial and screamed into the phone when I heard the voicemail again.

I started the engine a second time, but still, the car wouldn't move. Another scream escaped my lips as the zombie elf stared back at me. Or rather the back of his head did. Tears blurred my vision as I began swearing under my breath. I turned the key again, and the engine sputtered to life. "Thank you!"

Slamming the car into reverse, I mowed down two of the zombies as I backed out of the driveway. The third zombie, the one on the roof, toppled off but grabbed the handle on the driver's door. Thank goodness, I had the sense to lock all the doors. If this had been in my hometown with a bunch of cars on the road, I never would have been able to speed down the street like an Indy 500 racer.

The zombie hanging off my door began jiggling the handle. He wasn't the smartest creatures on the face of the planet because he did not do a single thing to stop me from almost clipping him with a mailbox. He let out an unearthly squeal as his arm tore from the rest of his body. When we got to the edge of my street, the zombie's arm fell off and rolled into the gutter.

A few minutes later, I raced into the driveway of the Van Helsing home. Eddie was running out the front door just as I stumbled out of the car. "Shelly, what happened to my car?" he asked as he saw the blood and gore all over the trunk's hood and on the driver's door.

My lips quivered for only a few minutes before I threw my arms around him. "Why didn't you answer your cell phone?" I shouted at him as hot tears stung my eyes and cheeks. "What is wrong with you? I called you four times, and you didn't answer!"

"I was on the phone," Eddie tried to explain, but I cut him off.

"I could have been killed! There were four of them, and they all wanted me dead!"

Eddie wrapped his arms around me and held me. Saying nothing, he let me cry against him. Once I was done, he gently asked me what happened.

"Zombies," I managed to say in a low voice as I wiped the remaining tears. I told him exactly what had happened to me back at my house. "But I don't think that they were ordinary zombies. The one whose head I took out with the fire extinguisher did not die!"

Eddie's face grew paler than normal. He began pacing back and forth in the gravel driveway. "Not good," he muttered. "Not good at all." He was alarmed somebody had set an enemy zombie curse on me. I didn't know what that it entailed, but it had to be bad because my boyfriend had no idea what to do about it.

"What's an enemy zombie curse, Eddie?" I asked.

He gave a nervous laugh. "Unfortunately, babe, all I know is that it's a very bad curse." Then he broke into a hopeful grin. "But I do know someone who does know!"

It was very quiet on the drive over to David Endora's home. From what I knew about David Endora, I felt somewhat better about this night. The wizard was the one who took my boyfriend in soon after he became a vampire. "So, when did David move here?" I asked Eddie.

"Earlier this week. He was the one I was on the phone with when you tried calling me." He paused for a moment and then said in a low voice, "I'm sorry, babe. I had no idea that you were in trouble."

I leaned against the window, shutting my eyes in a failed attempt to blot out the images of the zombies surrounding my house. I had nearly been killed this evening, and what good did my magical talent do for me? Other than alerting me zombies were out to shorten my lifespan. Oh, yeah, the ability to telecommunicate with the undead comes in real handy when you're battling zombies. I finally spoke, "I just wish I could've sent you a telepathic message." I paused again. "I hate my talent!"

We stopped at a red light, and Eddie looked at me in surprise. "What do you mean by that, Shelly? You have a great talent."

I shook my head. "Yeah, right. Since when has my talent ever saved a life? When we were stuck on the top of the Ferris wheel, who couldn't do anything to get us down? Me. When the demon attacked the diner six months ago, who couldn't do a thing to stop it? Me! I feel like Aquaman or even worse Zan from the Wonder Twins."

Eddie reached across the seat and gave my knee a gentle squeeze. "Shelly, you were the one who came up with a crazy, but very effective plan to defeat the demon. You also warned me about the zombies in the tunnel ride." I was about to argue at this point, but he continued. "Yes, your ability is limited, but you have another talent."

"What's that?" I asked, doubtfully.

"You're a regular MacGyver. You're always coming up with crazy ideas, and they always work out. It's one of the many things I love about you, Shelly." He laughed as he recalled a memory we had shared together. "I remember how you kicked Stregone's henchman's butt with your Kung Fu moves. You're smart, ingenious—."

"Ingenious, huh?"

"Oh, come on, Shelly. You're the only person I know who has beat back zombies with a fire extinguisher! I wish I could've seen you in action."

Every time I talk with Eddie about what's troubling me, he always cheers up. I then realized I hadn't told him everything that had happened today. By the time I was done with my tale, we were turning into the long, winding driveway of Eddie's friend, the wizard. "Wow!" I said as I stared up at the gorgeous two-story colonial. "This place is beautiful! Your friend has excellent taste."

"I'll tell him you said that!" Eddie put the car in park, and we walked up to the front oak door. He gave it a couple of raps.

The door opened. Dressed in a green leisure suit with a black dress shirt, David Endora greeted us. The wizard was just shy of three-hundred-years-old, but I barely noticed the specks of gray sprinkled in his dark brown hair. His iridescent eyes shifted to my boyfriend as he smiled warmly. "Eddie," he said, giving him a bear hug with his burly arms, "it's so good to see you again!"

"Same here!" Eddie replied as he returned the hug. "I see you're wearing that old leisure suit!"

"Actually, I pulled it out just for you," David said with a grin. Then he turned to me. "And you must be Shelly. Eddie couldn't stop talking about you!" He shook my hand with a firm shake.

"It's good to meet you, sir," I said.

"Oh, call me David!" He beckoned us into the foyer. I can always tell whenever I enter the home of a Welkie. Even though David had just moved here, you would never know it. There were no boxes anywhere to be seen, the walls had been freshly painted, and in fact, the entire house was in perfect condition. "So, Shelly, Eddie tells me you have zombie problems."

David's question brought me out of my awe. "Yeah, it's a long story."

"Well, we can discuss it in my study." David led us to the end of the hall into a large room with a snow-white carpet. The walls were lined with tall cherry bookcases filled with old books on spells and enchantments, the histories of various races, and many other magic-related subjects. David had us sit in green velvet chairs with high backs near one of the many bookcases while he went to the kitchen to get us some tea.

Once Eddie and I were left alone, I grabbed the vampire's hand. "He's such a gentleman," I said in a low voice. The atmosphere of the room made me want to whisper.

"Why do you think I respect him so much?" Eddie answered with a grin. "And don't worry, David will find a way to defeat the zombies."

David came back carrying a tray filled with three teacups, a boiling teapot, and a bowl overflowing with sugar. I huddled over the tea like a vulture. The wizard smiled at me as I poured

the tea into my cup. "I can see why you and Eddie are together.

You both have a very strong sweet tooth!"

I glanced down at the fourth spoonful of sugar that was

about to make the descent into my already sweetened

strawberry leaf tea. Maybe I was overdoing it. After I gave a

sheepish smile, I quickly sat down beside Eddie who had gotten

up for his tea. I didn't feel all that bad when Eddie put five scoops

of sugar into his cup. Upon David's request, I told him everything

that had transpired in the past few days.

He was very interested in the chicken head. "Was it

fresh?"

I nodded. "It was still leaking!" I happened to glance over

at Eddie who nearly spewed out his tea, although it wasn't that

hot! *Sorry about the visual image, Eddie*. He smiled sickly at me.

"Eddie thinks Ahab Boko might have cast an enemy zombie spell

on me."

David took a sip of his herbal tea and then set the cup

down before he got a book almost exactly like the one Eddie

found in the dumpster. He flipped through the book until he found the page he was looking for. He motioned for Eddie and me to see what he had found. "As you can see, an enemy zombie curse is the fifth-worst curse in magical history."

I couldn't resist. "What are the four worst?"

Eddie rolled his eyes at me. "What can you tell us about these kinds of zombies?" he asked his mentor, changing the course of the conversation.

"Well," David said, "for one thing, these kinds of zombies can't be killed by the usual way, like destroying the brains. The necromancer instructs the zombies to harm or kill only his sworn enemy."

I gulped. Sworn enemy? All I did was report Boko for being creepy and following me around in the stacks. I had now risen from telepathic librarian to sworn enemy of a kooky sorcerer.

"So, how do we stop them?" Eddie always knows to ask the most important question.

David sighed. "It depends on the necromancer. He might use something simple like a condiment!"

"You mean like ketchup and mustard?" I blurted out.

David smiled at me. "I've heard zombies under these kinds of curses can be defeated even by mayonnaise." He ignored the shocked looks on our faces and continued with the explanation. "Usually, it's a common household object that can somehow cover the place where the zombies first died."

"So, how can you tell what kills them?" I asked again. With my luck, I'd be dead before the zombie antidote would be found.

"If this sorcerer is organized at all, he might leave notes about the spell, but that's highly unlikely."

"Not the most effective way to perform a spell! Even I remember that from my classes at UCM." Eddie said softly.

David shot the vampire a skeptical look. "Does she know, Eddie?"

My boyfriend nodded. David hadn't known that I knew about Eddie's past. Only a small handful of people know how he had been turned, and I was one of those privileged people.

"Oh," David said in complete understanding. Nothing more was said about the zombies. Instead, David asked me a lot of questions about my family and background, how Eddie and I met, and many other questions. Finally, the Welkie walked us to the door. Eddie went to start the car.

I was about to follow him after we said our good-byes to David when he grabbed my arm. "Shelly," he said, "I'm so glad that Eddie has found you." He glanced over to where the love of my life was unlocking the driver's door. "I have known him for a long time, and even though he has had a few girlfriends in the past, I can tell he's very much in love with you. For him to divulge his past is not something he does often. Call it an old wizard's premonition, but I have a feeling you two will be together for a long time."

I must have blushed when I thanked him. He was right. Eddie was certainly in love with me, and me with him. Even though I had stumbled upon my boyfriend's past on my own, I knew in my heart, Eddie and I were meant to be together. I climbed in the passenger seat and gave my boyfriend a kiss on the lips.

He raised an eyebrow in surprise. "Whoa! What was that for? Not that I'm objecting or anything."

"Just because I love you, Eddie!"

He returned the kiss. "I love you, too, Shelly!" He put the

car in reverse and off we went. As we turned out of David's driveway, Eddie spotted someone walking along the other side of the street. "Hey, it's Boko!" He pushed down on the top of my head, ruining my perfect braid. "Get down! I don't want him seeing you!"

"No need to tell me twice," I said. Because I'm so short (five-foot-one-and-half), I only had to push the seat back a few inches so that I could get all the way down to the dirty floor. Even though Eddie had cleaned up my vomit, there was still a faint smell. What I wouldn't give to have a bottle of air freshener handy?

Then an idea came to me. Actually, it was more like a brilliant, yet dangerous idea. Well, I was already the object of a zombie curse, so how else could I endanger my life? "Let's follow him!"

Chapter Twelve:
We Break into Another Sorcerer's Home

Eddie and I sat in the car only a few feet away from the abandoned house where we had seen my stalker enter. The headlights were turned off so the sorcerer couldn't see us. In fact, Boko had been in there for over an hour. "So, this is the essence of a stakeout?" I asked the former spy/bounty hunter. I had crawled out from my cramped hiding place.

Eddie raised an eyebrow. "Come on, Shelly, didn't your dad ever tell you how boring stakeouts are? Nothing happens!" He was right. Dad had been a police officer for twenty years and never once enjoyed hanging out in a patrol car during a stakeout. I leaned against Eddie's shoulder and rested my eyes as we waited for something to happen at the shabby house. "Good point!"

Eddie put an arm around me. "Well, you were the one

who wanted to follow him," he said with a smile. "It's a shame no one else wanted to go zombie hunting with us!"

I had made several phone calls, inviting Robin, Brooke, and some of our other friends, but they had all refused my offer. "I know! Philistines!"

Eddie decided to change the topic. "So, have you decided what to do about Jordan?"

"I don't know. I don't have the money for her operation, but I don't want her to be put to sleep." I threw my hands up in frustration as a great sigh escaped from my lips. Unfortunately, even in a magical land like Zephyr, money doesn't grow on trees.

"Shelly, if you want, I'd be more than willing to help foot the bill."

"No!" I balked. It wasn't that Eddie didn't have the money, I just didn't want him to feel like he had to help me with the vet's bill. "Don't worry about it. I'll figure out a way!"

"Are you sure?" he asked. "Because it won't be a problem, and don't worry about paying me back."

"Look, Eddie, I appreciate the offer." Eddie gave me a hurt look. "I really do, but I want to handle this on my own. I bought her and have taken care of her all by myself, and I don't need any help!"

The vampire gave a defeated sigh. He knows I can be stubborn sometimes, especially with money. He turned to look out the windshield as he crossed his arms.

I touched his arm. "Eddie, I didn't mean to hurt your feelings. It's just there are some things I need to handle on my own."

He didn't say anything for his eyes were focused on the front porch. "Shh! He's about to leave!"

I looked out at the porch. Boko was saying something, but we couldn't tell what exactly. Then he turned around in our direction. I slid back down in my seat while Eddie turned himself into mist. A few agonizing seconds slowly ticked by as we waited breathlessly for the sorcerer to come and most likely blow us up. Gathering up my courage, I peered over the hood of the car. "Where did he go?" I asked.

Eddie materialized and quickly glanced up and down the street. "I don't know! Weren't you watching him?"

"No! I thought you were!"

We sat in the car for a few more moments before Eddie opened his door. "Well, now that he's gone, I guess we can check out his house."

I followed him as he crossed the street towards the seemingly abandoned house. The pink paint was peeling off, revealing a hidden coat of orange. Every single windowpane was broken. I stepped onto the lawn which had been converted into the Amazon jungle over the years as Eddie sprinted up onto the decaying porch. He ventured over to the front door and had barely brushed up against the doorknob when a bright yellow flash of energy bolted forward, knocking him off his feet. He landed on his rear in a pile of tangled dandelions and clovers.

"Eddie, are you okay?" I ran over to him and helped him to his feet.

He gratefully took my hand, regretting the fact he had forgotten to check to see if there was a ward put on the house. Wards are a type of protection spells that can be placed around any objects for long periods of time. It's a great home security system because only the person(s) who set it can disarm the spell. "My butt's going to hurt for a bit!" he said with a smile.

I placed my hands on my hips and looked at the ugly house. "So now what?"

"Well, most of the time, Welkies don't set a ward on their entire house," Eddie said as we walked around to the back of the house. He spotted a wooden rollaway door that was covered with huge holes chewed by either termites or mice both being the size of Utah. Eddie let out a gentle ball of energy at the door to see if the ward would bounce off the spell before. We both held our breath and waited. Nothing happened. Eddie released the breath he had been holding. "All right, let's go!"

I grabbed one of the rusted handles while my boyfriend grabbed the other one. On the count of three, we heaved back both doors. The creaky wooden stairs led into the inky darkness of the cellar. I grabbed the crook of the vampire's elbow after he retrieved his flashlight from his magic kit. We then descended the stairs with the flashlight casting eerie shadows on the walls. Everything went great until we reached the bottom of the stairs. That's when something furry brushed across my bare legs. I gave a shriek of terror.

Eddie dropped the flashlight on the ground. "Shelly, what's

the matter?" he asked.

"Something furry is in here!" I said as I pulled down on Eddie's shoulder.

"I'm sure it's nothing, babe," he assured me as he scooped up the flashlight. Moving it around, he let the beam rest on a dark area. A pair of yellow eyes stared back at us.

"It's a rat! A huge, disgusting rat!" I gasped. If there is one thing that freaks me out, it's rats.

"Are you too scared to look in here?" Eddie asked. "Because we can just leave."

"No," I replied in a shaky voice. "Let me get on your back!"

"What?"

"You're strong and you can carry me on your back until we reach the stairs. And I'll even carry the flashlight for you."

"Fine, fine! Just to make you happy." The vampire squatted down and let me climb on his back. Then he grabbed my legs as he straightened himself up. I must have leaned too far back because I almost crushed his Adam's apple with my arms.

"Giddyup!" I ordered as the flashlight I was holding cut a

path through the darkness.

"Watch it or Horsy here will buck you off!" Eddie replied as he carried me through the dank basement.

We finally found the cellar stairs. It was all too quiet on the home front. "This was way too easy."

"You'd think that Boko would put a ward around his entire house, knowing your track record," Eddie added with a grin. "Come to think of it, this is the second time you have broken into a sorcerer's home." He felt around for something to hold onto, in case the stairs decided to collapse under our combined weight. He found the wooden railing and gently avoided getting any splinters as he walked up the stairs.

"Technically, this is the first time because Stregone invited us into his home."

"Right, right!" Eddie replied as he opened up the door at the top of the basement stairs. He set me down, and we walked into a dimly lit hallway.

"Where would a Welkie keep all his stuff to do magic?" I asked in a low voice. The last thing we needed was to be chased away by zombies. I was pretty sure Boko left a few of them here to dispose of any intruders.

"Look for a cluttered table," Eddie whispered back. It only took us a few moments to find a cramped room with a little cluttered table. Huge, old dust covers lay on the floor in a pile. There wasn't any chair anywhere in the room which puzzled me. Even I liked to sit down every once in a while.

Eddie was pushing back scribbled-on notepaper, empty junk food bags, and other mess which covered the table. I began helping him. "Just what exactly are we looking for?" I asked him.

He thought for a minute or two before he spoke. "If I remember from my schooling, most people will write down the thing which can stop a zombie, if they can't be killed the usual way."

I glanced around until I spotted a piece of paper with lots of scribbles. The words, fire, holy water, and brimstone were scribbled out vigorously. The only word left on the paper was salt, scrawled in big letters and underlined several times. In one aspect of his life, Boko was a lot like me, writ. I shivered at the scary thought. "Yes," I almost shouted. "Salt! I think this is the zombie's kryptonite!" I stuffed the piece of paper into the pocket of my jeans.

Eddie clamped a hand over my mouth again. "Shelly, have you lost your mind?" he said in a whisper. "No doubt Boko has zombies guarding the house."

"Sorry." I whispered back as I removed his hand from my mouth. A familiar address written on a sticky note caught my eye. I was about to mention it when we both heard noises coming from the hallway. The vampire grabbed my hand and pulled me with him under the table.

The lurching stopped inside the doorway of our room, and my heart stopped beating momentarily. The thoughts I was receiving told me there were three zombies with Eddie and me. How were we going to get out of this mess with the unstoppable living dead?

Shelly, Eddie interrupted my thoughts, *we have to get out of here now!*

Do you have any bright ideas?

Eddie shook his head. He drew me close to protect me from the things that were about to attack us. Then an idea, a somewhat effective one, came to him. He let go of me and gave the table one good shove. The table went flying at the zombies.

I watched in horror as the vampire's great strength caused the table to slice the zombies in half. Then, what scared me most was the upper torso of one of them began using its arms to drag itself across the floor towards us. I let out a terrified scream. "Eddie, do something!"

"Stay behind me!" he ordered as he began to whip up a couple of fireball spells. Once he gave the word, two white balls of fire shot out from his hands at rapid speed. The only good they did was send the zombies and their parts back out of the room, screaming pain from the third-degree burns. Eddie grabbed my hand and began to drag me towards one of the windows.

"What-what—what are you going to do?" I stammered as I looked back at the door half expecting the zombies to reappear at any minute.

Eddie answered my question by throwing a powerful energy spell at a boarded-up window. Splinters flew outside onto the knee-high grass. "Come on, Shelly!" he shouted. He leaped out of the open window and landed safely on the ground.

I was about to follow him when a hand grabbed my ankle and pulled me to the hardwood floor. "Eddie!" I screamed as the disembodied hand dragged me towards the door. The zombie hand was very strong as it dragged me into the hallway. The three guardian zombies were near the cellar door. Where was Eddie? I screamed for him again.

This wouldn't be how it ended. I wasn't going to be eaten alive by ravenous zombie clowns. I snatched up a candlestick that had fallen to the floor in the madness. I repeatedly slammed my weapon down on the disembodied wrist. Nothing happened.

Suddenly, a green mist enveloped me. Eddie appeared in front of me, his concealed guns drawn like a cowboy from the Old West. He began firing right at the heads of the zombies, drawing them back. "Out the window!" he ordered. "Now!"

I gave the zombie's hand one last smash with the candlestick, and I was finally free. I climbed out the broken window and jumped safely to the ground. Eddie soon followed, and we both booked it to the car.

"I think we're safe!" Eddie said, once we were safe in the confines of his carrot car. "You okay, babe?"

I nodded. "Just shaken up, that's all." Then I remembered another note I had seen on the table. "Eddie, we have to get to my dad's, now!"

"Why?"

"I saw my dad's address in that clutter of papers. Boko might send his zombie hoard after Dad."

"Okay!" Eddie said with a nod. He started the engine. "Buckle up. It's going to be a wild ride!"

We arrived at Dad's in less than two minutes. After getting out of the car, I followed Eddie around to the back where he popped the trunk. "So, what's our zombie arsenal like?"

The vampire handed me a tire iron. "This should fend them off!"

"What about you?"

"Don't worry about me. I can handle them." He pulled out his black duffle bag filled with various weapons and slung it over his shoulder. "Your dad has a shotgun, right?"

I looked at him. "My dad's an ex-cop, remember? Of course, he does."

We paraded up to the back door, and Eddie gave four, sharp knocks while I played lookout.

"I'm coming! I'm coming!" Dad shouted from inside. "Who is it?"

"It's Shelly and Eddie," I answered.

Dad unlocked the door and greeted us in his red bathrobe wrapped loosely around his red and white striped pajamas. "What on earth are you two doing here at this hour?"

I glanced at my watch. It was almost eleven-thirty. "Um, Eddie and I were in the neighborhood, and we thought we would ask how the wedding plans were coming along," I said as the vampire and I moved quickly inside, quickly locking the door behind us.

"Why do you have a tire iron in your hand, Shelly?" Dad asked.

"Oh that!" I said mentally debating how to break the news gently. "I like tire irons." The weak lie fell hesitantly off my tongue. Screw it. "Let's all sit down."

"We'll have a better vantage point from the living room," Eddie remarked as he ushered my stunned father into the living room where I began drawing the curtains.

"Your front door has a locked deadbolt, right, Mr. Anderson?" Eddie placed his weapons bag on the coffee table. He unzipped it and took out a vaporizer gun. "Oh, crap! I should've fully charged this thing earlier."

"Whoa! Whoa! What is going on here?" Dad looked at us in astonishment.

"Dad, you might need a gun."

"Why?"

"Shelly is the object of an enemy zombie curse, and apparently, the zombies know your address," Eddie explained.

"Lovely!" Dad said, fully accepting the madness. "I'll be right back." He ran upstairs and was back in a few minutes fully dressed and armed with his .38 and .357. "These things should take out the zombies," he said.

"Maybe," I said.

"What do you mean 'maybe'?" Dad asked.

"Let's just say these zombies don't die the conventional way," Eddie explained.

"Then how should we go about defending ourselves?"

Dad asked. "Shelly, did you get a chance to use your telepathy on them?"

I rolled my eyes before I went into a sarcastic diatribe. "Oh, yes, Dad! I got really connected to the minds of those flesh-eating zombies. And you know what? They divulged their greatest weaknesses."

"Shelly, don't be smart," Dad said, irritably, but Eddie shot me a quick, fanged grin.

"Ooh," I said, remembering the zombie's kryptonite. "I'll be right back!" I sprinted into my father's kitchen and began rooting around in the cabinets.

"Dad!" I shouted. "Where do you keep your salt?"

"In the cupboard above the fridge!" he shouted back.

"Found it!" I pulled down the large container of salt and shook it. Crap! It was almost empty. I shook my head. "It'll have to do." I went back to the living room. Eddie was crouched by the huge picture window and was loading a round of laser bullets into his Scorpion XL handgun. I crept over to him and picked up my weapon. "How come you get a gun, and I get a lousy tire iron?"

"Because you're a horrible shot," he responded.

"You only saw me that one time at the shooting range."

"Yeah, and you missed the target by a good five-feet."

"It was at night!"

"We were using laser bullets."

"Good point."

Dad joined us as he put away his cell phone. "I just called Amelia and told her to stay hidden." He stretched his arm across the entire room and dimmed the lights.

"Good idea," Eddie replied. He looked over at me. "Are they here yet?"

"Hello! Physical barrier," I said pointing to the wall. "Limits my telepathy."

"Oops, sorry!" Eddie said sheepishly.

Just then the doorbell rang, throwing us off guard. Who would be ringing doorbells at this hour of the night? I peeked out the window. "Oh, this is totally not fair!" I complained. "How come Dad gets the polite zombies?"

Eddie glanced out the window. "Because it seems Boko not only raised dead clowns, but also, four door-to-door salesmen!"

"Are you sure?" I asked. My question was answered when an old, dirt-encrusted briefcase came crashing through the front door at top speed. With the way cleared, the zombies lurched into the house.

Dad blasted away at two of them with his .357 magnum, and Eddie hurled a huge energy spell at another one. A fourth one in a tattered suit swiped a rotting hand at me. "Shelly!" my boyfriend shouted.

"Don't worry about me!" I shouted back. "Heads up!" I told the zombie. I swung the tire iron like a baseball bat and whacked its head off at the shoulders.

Dad looked at me in shock. "Wow, Shelly! Usually, you don't have the stomach for this."

"It's okay," I assured him. "I'll probably throw up later."

Eddie shot a fanged grin at me as he drove a zombie back outside with his gun.

We watched in alarm as the injured, living dead hoard slowly put themselves back together to their original grotesque state. "Have we forgotten these zombies don't die the conventional ways?" I asked.

Then I remembered the salt. Their kryptonite! But what to do, what to do? A plan began to form in my mind. I stepped outside, salt can in hand. I could hear Dad and Eddie telling me to get back inside, but I ignored them. "Cover me!" I uncapped the lid and began flinging salt at the oncoming dead salesmen.

The mineral landed in their eyes, and they began to freeze as if they were statues. I was about to fling some more at them when Dad yanked me back inside.

"What were you thinking?" Dad shouted.

"Well, I was trying to help!" I pointed out.

"You could've been killed!"

I pointed to the zombie statues. "I just saved our lives. Give me a little credit, Dad."

"Everyone stand back!" Eddie ordered. He shut his eyes, held out his hands, palms up, and shouted in an authoritative voice, "Contengo house!" A surge of magic erupted from the vampire's open palms. A green force field surrounded the outside of the house and faded into a transparent dome-like shape. This was the first time I had ever seen Eddie cast a ward spell, and let me tell you, it was impressive. That is, until he nearly collapsed to the floor from sheer exhaustion.

Dad and I helped him onto the couch. "You okay, hon?" I asked the vampire.

Eddie nodded. "Yeah, that spell took a lot out of me. But it should hold off the rest of the zombies, at least for tonight."

"And what about you two?" Dad asked. "I don't want you out there with those zombies on the loose, Shelly."

"Oh, Dad," I said, "you don't need to worry about us. Eddie and I can take care of ourselves."

My father crossed his arms over his chest. "And what will you do if those zombies attack your house while you sleep."

I shook off his concern with a wave of my hand. "I'm a light sleeper so I'll hear them coming. All I need is a good weapon. A sword would be kind of cool."

Eddie wearily shook his head at me as his energy slowly returned. "We wouldn't be able to leave here anyway."

"Why is that?" Dad asked.

"Because the spell will only work if I remain in the house."

"But what about Boko's house," I asked. "He wasn't there,

and yet the ward on his house was still in place."

"That's because it was his property. When a wizard casts a ward spell on something he owns, he doesn't have to be near it all the time."

"So, when a ward spell is placed on something he doesn't own, for instance, this house, the wizard has to stay nearby?" Dad asked.

Eddie nodded. "If I leave here, the spell will instantly wear off."

Dad blew out a sigh. "I guess you're both sleeping here tonight. Eddie, let's get you set up with the air mattress down in the basement, if that's okay."

My boyfriend pushed himself off the couch. "Yeah, sure," he said. "No problem, Mr. Anderson." He followed my father down to the basement rec room.

I peeked out the shattered window before heading to the upstairs bathroom. Lo and behold, the non-petrified zombies had left. It was safe for now. I shook my head at the disheveled living room. It looked like a demilitarized zone with all the bullet holes, blood, and brains everywhere. Good thing Dad doesn't rent because any landlord would have him evicted on the spot, I pondered. I glanced back outside and took one quick look up and down the dark, empty street. Either my father had the worst neighbors ever or they had all been terrified by the lurking zombies. I was banking on the latter.

I went upstairs to my old bedroom and grabbed an old blue T-shirt and pink-and-blue, striped pajama bottoms I had stashed in an emergency overnight dresser drawer, complete with a set of casual and work clothes. I went into the bathroom and took a good look at myself in the bathroom mirror. I looked like Nellie Lovett from Sweeney Todd with my bloodstained shirt. But the funny thing was I didn't feel sick as the memories of the last hour resurfaced in my mind. My stomach was getting stronger, or I was slowly becoming desensitized to carnage. I hoped it was not the latter.

I heard a knock on the door. "Shelly?" Eddie called. "Everything okay?"

"Yeah, I'm fine," I said as I unlocked and opened the door. "I'm just going to take a quick shower before going to bed."

He looked down at my shirt. "And change out of the

bloody outfit, I hope?"

"Yep, that's my plan."

"Here, if you give me your shirt, I'll throw it in the wash for you."

"Sure, give me a second," I closed the door and quickly changed into a clean shirt. Once I opened the door, I tossed the bloodstained shirt to Eddie. "Thanks, hon."

"You're welcome," he said, but there was something else on his mind. "About what happened at Boko's," he said in a voice low enough for my ears only. "I'm so sorry."

It took me a few seconds to figure out what he talking about. "It's all right, Eddie."

"No, it's not. I should've made sure you got out first. I don't know what I was thinking."

I put my hand on his shoulder. "We got out of there safely. That's all that matters."

"I know," he said softly, "but back there I thought I was going to lose you. If anything ever happened to you, I would never forgive myself."

I wrapped my arms around his waist and leaned against

him. "Same here."

"You're right though. We're okay, and that's all that matters." He looked over at my dad who was coming up the stairs.

"Good night, you two!" Dad said.

"Night, Dad."

"Night, Mr. Anderson." We waited for my father to shut his bedroom door behind him before we continued our conversation. "You sure you're all right, Shelly?"

"I'll be fine, Eddie. Don't worry."

"By the way, that was some sweet zombie fighting back there."

"All adrenaline, dear, all adrenaline. So, what are we going to do about our little zombie problem?"

"Don't know. I was kind of hoping you had a plan."

"Me? Why me?"

"Because in this relationship, you're the brains, and I'm the brawn."

I grinned widely and gave him a fist bump. "True dat. But why don't we both go to bed and try to come up with a workable plan in the morning?"

"Sounds good," Eddie said. We kissed goodnight and went to bed.

Chapter Thirteen:
I Pull a MacGyver

The alarm clock on my cell phone beeped at six-thirty in the morning. I woke up, forgetting for a minute where I was. I was about to fall back asleep when I heard a knock on my door.

"Shelly, it's Dad. Do you want me to take you to work today?"

"Thanks, Dad! Can we leave at eight?"

"No problem. There's a towel in the bathroom for you." He turned and padded down the hall to his bedroom.

I finally dragged my butt out of bed. As I showered, I thought about what had transpired in the past few days. There had to be something I could do to stop the zombies. "Think Shelly! You can come up with something," I told myself as I rubbed the conditioner in. What would MacGyver do? He had been in lots of scrapes, but I was pretty sure he never dealt with indestructible zombies. Okay, I knew that the zombies could be destroyed with salt, evident by what happened last night. Now, I just needed a plan that would work with salt. Slowly, my brain started formulating a plan. Yes, it was dangerous, and if it was in a yearbook, it would be voted most likely not to succeed.

I finished getting ready, pulled my hair back into a wet ponytail, and ran down to the basement. My boyfriend was sleeping soundly under a couple of blankets atop the air mattress. "Eddie, wake up," I said as I got down on my knees and shook his shoulder.

He woke with a start. "What's going on?" he asked, thinking the zombies had somehow gotten past the ward.

"How late were you up, Eddie?" I asked.

"Late, Shelly? I just went to bed an hour ago!" He had a valid point. Vampires sleep during the day. So, in fact, he didn't stay up at all. He repeated his first question.

"I have an idea on how we can get rid of the zombies." As soon as I finished telling my plan, I waited expectantly for Eddie's response. "So, what do you think?"

He had propped himself up on his elbows and was now

raising a skeptical eyebrow at me. Finally, he spoke. "It's dangerous, but I think it'll work. I'll pick you up after work so we can get the stuff you need."

"You're the best, Eddie," I said as I gave him a kiss on the lips. "Rest up!" I waved good-bye to him and watched the vampire throw the covers back over his head. When I read his mind, I was reminded how much he loved me. He had been on the alert for the zombies until the sun had risen about five o'clock. What a great guy!

Eddie picked me up a little after six that evening. The first stop was to Buy-A-Bundle, a store where one can buy items in bulk. Dad always gets restaurant supplies there. I grabbed a cart, and Eddie and I headed for Aisle Six where all the seasonings and condiments were. "So," I asked Eddie as I looked at the two-gallon containers in front of me, "how many things of salt do you think we need?"

"I don't know, Shelly," Eddie said with a shrug. He was leaning against the shopping cart's handle. "Did you get a measurement of the area where the building was burned down?"

I nodded. "Yeah, I did a little research on my lunch break."

I gave him the dimensions that I had written down on a piece of paper. He glanced at it and did a quick, mental calculation. "I'm guessing we're going to need about five bottles."

"Well, let's get at least ten. Just to make sure we have enough." I began handing containers to Eddie who placed them in the cart. "I've asked Robin if I could borrow Cornelius for the job. He said he'd meet us with Brooke."

"Spreading salt over zombie graves. Now that's romantic!"

"We can't do this by ourselves," I said as we headed to the front to pay for our purchases. "Speaking of romance, you know what date is coming up, Eddie?"

My boyfriend shook his head. "Your dad's marriage?" he ventured.

"No, our six-month anniversary is next week."

"Oh!"

"You forgot, didn't you?"

Eddie gave a nervous laugh. He mentally reprimanded himself for already doing the typical guy thing: forgetting important dates. "To tell you the truth, yes." He paused slightly.

"So, where do you want to go?"

I didn't have to think about that one. "What about that restaurant, Ambrosia? I've heard it has great food." I gave him my best Bambi eyes.

"We'll see," Eddie said mysteriously. When the cashier had rung up our purchases, I realized that I didn't have enough money. He came to the rescue and paid the remaining balance.

Brooke and Robin met us at the entrance to the fairgrounds. My brother eyed the containers of salt I was dumping into the garbage bags that I had asked him to bring. "Is this really going to work, Shelly?" he asked.

"Of course, it is," I said, trying to keep an upbeat, confident tone in my voice.

"I thought you could just get rid of the zombies by destroying their brains," Brooke mentioned.

Eddie shook his head. "Not these zombies. Boko has made them almost invincible."

Robin looked at me. "You really should stop hanging out with freaky people."

I rolled my eyes at him. "You're so funny I forgot to laugh." I looked up from my work to see a small group of people walking towards us. "What are they doing here?

"I've asked Dirk, Lisa, Roger, and Strider to help us out!" Robin explained.

I looked at my brother. "What?" I asked. "You shouldn't have asked them. All I need is to borrow Cornelius. Eddie and I don't need any more help."

"What's this I hear, you don't want our help?" Lisa asked as she and the others approached.

"I don't want to get you guys involved in my problems," I explained. I grabbed one of the bags and lugged it towards my brother's dragon.

"Shelly, stop being so stubborn!" Lisa said as she placed her hands on her hips.

"Yeah, you need help," Roger said to me. "Lisa can provide some light, I can dump some salt while Strider is guiding Lucky, Dirk can do the same with Robin's help and Eddie can direct Cornelius for you."

Eddie held up his hands at that one. "Sorry, Roger," he

said to Lisa's twin brother, "I don't do flying!" Flying is the one thing that gives my guy motion sickness.

"Actually, I can give better light if I'm up high," Lisa said.

"Okay," Roger replied. He ran his hands though his fiery red hair as he carefully rethought his plan. "How about you and I take Lucky?" he suggested to Lisa. "Robin, you and Brooke take Cornelius, and Dirk and Strider take Ringo."

"Got it!" Dirk and Strider said together.

I had stopped listening to everyone trying to take over my job because I was too busy reading the minds of the forty zombie clowns, who were coming in our direction "Uh, guys!"

"Not now, Shelly," Roger replied as he and everyone else began forming plans to get rid of the zombies.

Nobody was listening to me! "We have a slight problem," I said. Still, no one paid attention. "There are about forty zombies heading our way!"

"Are you sure?" Brooke asked me.

"Positive," I replied. "They're coming from the north." I pointed toward the direction of where I had read their minds.

"Actually, that's south, babe!" Eddie said as he gently

turned me in the right direction.

"Whatever! But we need to change our plans."

"How so?" Strider asked me.

I swallowed hard as I began rapidly to put together another plan. "We need to spread a good amount of the salt where the zombies are going to be so they will walk right into it! Then I'll somehow lure the zombies towards the trap!"

"Will that work?" Dirk asked in an uncertain tone.

I looked around at everyone's skeptical faces and then looked to my boyfriend for support. "I'm all for it," he said. Your plan will work, babe, and I'm going with you.

I had everyone grab a bag of salt, and we began dumping it out evenly in a ten-by-ten-foot area. Once that was done, I ran towards the zombies with Eddie by my side. "I'm scared, Eddie," I admitted.

"I'll admit that I am too," Eddie replied as he kept pace with me. "But don't worry. I'm with you every step of the way, MacGyver."

We stopped a few feet away from the zombies who were lurching towards us. Behind the army was Boko. My blood boiled as I tensed in anger. That guy had nearly killed me on several

occasions, ruined my future stepmother's bridal shower and

injured my winged horse. Now it was my turn to ruin his life.

"Hey, worm breath!" I shouted at the zombies. "You want me?

Come and get me!"

The zombie clowns turned their rotten heads and glared

at me with their lifeless eyes. "Get her!" Boko ordered his army.

They started stumbling towards Eddie and me at an alarmingly

fast rate. The sorcerer somehow had made them faster, but not

brighter.

The vampire and I turned around and ran back towards to

where our friends. "Get back as far as you can!" I ordered

everyone as Eddie and I ran through the salt field.

The first five zombies had no idea what hit them when

they stepped onto the salt. The salt slowly began traveling up

their legs as it encased them in a stature-like state. Their

screams were covered as the salt entered their mouths,

releasing a crinkling cellophane-like sound. The creatures

quickly collapsed into a pile of shapeless dust and salt. I

breathed a huge sigh of relief as all forty things were destroyed.

But there was still the matter of Boko who seemed to have disappeared amidst all the excitement. "Where did he go?" Eddie asked as we all frantically looked around for the AWOL Welkie.

Using his molekines, Roger gathered up a pile of salt in the air. Apparently, he was hoping to toss it in the direction of the sorcerer. Both Brooke and Robin had their guns out. Strider and Dirk ran over to Ringo, Dirk's dragon and began searching the grounds from a bird's eye view of the park with Lisa lighting up the skies.

I did my part looking for Boko, wishing my telepathy wasn't limited to just the minds of the undead. I was trying to figure out where he might be when an invisible force threw me to the ground, nearly knocking the wind out of me. I screamed in surprise.

Boko materialized on top of me, pinning me to the ground. An ancient dagger with a serrated double-blade was held high in his left hand. "Usurper!" he screamed as he began to bring it down.

I barely heard Eddie call my name, but I saw him running towards me. He wasn't going to make it in time. Balling both of my hands in fists, I brought them up as fast and hard as I could until they connected with Boko's temples. He dropped the knife with a scream of terrific pain and clutched his head in his hands. I drove one of my knees into his crotch and then shoved him off, hard and fast. He let out another screech of pain as he rolled off me.

"Why did you attack my girlfriend?" Eddie growled as he lifted Boko off the ground by his throat.

"By order of my queen!" Boko slurred as his eyes began to glaze over. "I was ordered to kill the usurper to the crown!"

Okay, this guy was definitely the conductor of the crazy train. I got up from the ground and brushed myself off the best I could. "Who is the queen?" I demanded.

Boko smirked "Not you!" he said with a laugh and coughed up a little blood. "And there's nothing you can do about it." But he stopped smirking when Eddie applied a little more pressure on my stalker's Adam's apple.

A fanged smile crossed Eddie's face. "I could easily crush your windpipe with no effort whatsoever, but that would be pretty messy!"

Boko turned very pale at that suggestion. "What are my other options?"

"I could nail you below the belt again, but this time, it'll be much harder," I offered.

Eddie looked at me proudly. "You should be very afraid of her," he warned Boko.

"Actually," Robin said, trying to intervene. "I think we should take him to a hospital before arresting him."

"Yeah," Brooke agreed. "I think Shelly may have given him a concussion."

"Eddie, let him go," Robin ordered as he pulled out his cell phone to call 9-1-1.

The vampire dropped him to the ground with a THUD. He came over to me and put his arms around me. "Are you okay?" he whispered.

I leaned into him. "Fine, now that's over."

"Nice job getting rid of those zombies, Shelly," Dirk said, giving me a high five. "How did you figure it out? "As I excitedly told everyone what had happened, I was thinking about the conversation I had with Eddie the night before. He was right. My plan didn't go quite the way I had planned, but hey, it worked. *Wow, Shelly*, I said to myself as I surveyed the piles of zombie dust, *I guess you are a regular MacGyver.*

A few days later, I was standing in front of my bathroom mirror as I smoothed my black cocktail dress. Eddie called me the day before and told me to get dressed up for our date tonight. "I wonder where he's taking me," I called out to Lisa who was sitting at the kitchen table working on a client's wedding arrangements.

"Probably some place very nice!" she replied. She came into the bathroom. "Ooh, Shelly! Eddie will love that dress on you!" Suddenly, she reached into her pocket and handed me one of Eddie's checks. "He wanted you to have this so you could pay for Jordan's operation!"

"I told him that I didn't want him to pay for it!" I said.

"Actually, it's not just from Eddie. It's from your dad, Amelia, Dirk, Dad, Strider, Robin, and me. We all wanted to help."

I stared at the check. Eddie was right. I had been

stubborn, thinking I could somehow take care of things, like my injured winged horse, all on my own. I gave Lisa a big hug. "Thanks so much!"

We heard the front door open, and my boyfriend say, "Shelly, are you ready to go?"

Lisa dragged me out of the bathroom where Eddie was waiting for me. He was wearing a black suit with a black tie and white dress shirt, and he looked smoking hot! "Wow!" he said as he looked at me up and down. "You look beautiful in that dress!"

I blushed. "Thanks, you're not so bad-looking yourself!" Then I remembered the medium-sized box sitting on the kitchen table. "I got you that box of chocolates I promised you."

Eddie perked up. "Ooh, chocolate!" he said. Then he remembered the item he was holding behind his back to surprise me. "Happy six-month anniversary!" he said as he produced a dozen purple and white striped roses, my favorite kind of flowers.

I deeply inhaled the gorgeous scent. "They're beautiful, Eddie."

"I'll put those in water for you, Shelly!" Lisa said as she took the flowers from me.

"And one more thing," my boyfriend said as he reached into his jacket pocket and pulled out a black rectangular jewelry box. "Open it up!" he said, passing it to me.

I quickly complied as gave a small gasp as I gazed at the turquoise necklace against the silver lining. It was the same one I had fallen in love with at the mall. "Oh, Eddie, it's lovely." I grabbed his tie, pulled him closer, and kissed him deeply on the lips. He put the necklace around my neck and fastened the clasp. I kissed him once again.

Eddie slowly stepped back after he returned my kiss. "We'd better get going so we don't miss our reservations at Ambrosia, and then it's off to the planetarium."

"Sounds romantic," I told him. And it was.

COMING SOON

Holiday of the Undead

My Life Among the Undead: Book 5

It's almost Christmas in Zephyr. Everyone is trying to get ready for Timothy Anderson's wedding, but his daughter, Shelly Anderson, has her own problems to deal with. For one thing, Shelly has a really bad cold, and the expired medicine is making her see things. Or has the creepy doll our intrepid heroine is holding for a friend really come alive? Unfortunately, no one believes her about the doll, not even her boyfriend, the dashing vampire Eddie Van Helsing. This holiday season has a lot of strange questions for Shelly. Why is Eddie acting so secretive? Where did Shelly's deceased mother's wedding ring go? Did someone steal Eddie's prized car? Is the doll really alive, or is it a figment of Shelly's overstressed imagination? Can Shelly find Eddie the perfect Christmas gift? So, bring out the eggnog, string the lights, and play some jingle bells because it's sure to be a Christmas to remember.

About the Author

Camara Bragdon has her master's degree in library and information science and lives in Maine. This is the fourth book in her vampire series, *My Life among the Undead*.

www.camarambragdonauthor.com

www.ingramcontent.com/pod-product-compliance
Lightning Source LLC
Chambersburg PA
CBHW060419310726
48976CB00003B/1111